"Well,

B.J. waited for Derek's mirth to run its course.

She watched him through narrowed eyes. His well-worn sweats lovingly draped his lean frame, and B.J. could see his big toe sticking out of a hole in his sock.

For some reason, that hole, that naked toe, made B.J. want to cry. It said so much to her. It spoke of vulnerability, of being alone and of not being able to cope. It tugged her heart.

It scared her to death.

"You shouldn't have come," she whispered.

"Yes, I should." Derek moved closer. "I wanted to apologize for taking advantage this afternoon."

"Nothing happened."

"A kiss happened, B.J."

"One you've apologized for."

"No." Derek gently touched the back of his hand to her cheek. "I apologized for taking advantage, not for the kiss. Never for the kiss."

Dear Reader,

It's July, and at Silhouette Romance we have the perfect accompaniment to a day at the beach or a lazy afternoon in the backyard—six fabulous love stories that bring together the best possible happy-ever-afters and the most gorgeous heroes you can imagine. These handsome, caring men definitely have forever in mind!

July also continues our WRITTEN IN THE STARS series. Each month in 1992, we're proud to present a book that focuses on the hero and his astrological sign. This month we're featuring the passionate, protective Cancer man in Diana Whitney's utterly charming *The Last Bachelor*.

In months to come, watch for Silhouette Romance novels by your all-time favorites, including Diana Palmer, Suzanne Carey, Annette Broadrick and Brittany Young.

The Silhouette Romance authors and editors love to hear from readers, and we'd love to hear from *you*.

Until next month...happy reading!

Valerie Susan Hayward
Senior Editor

ANNE PETERS

Nobody's Perfect

Silhouette Romance

Published by Silhouette Books New York

America's Publisher of Contemporary Romance

If you purchased this book without a cover you should be aware that this book is stolen property. It was reported as "unsold and destroyed" to the publisher, and neither the author nor the publisher has received any payment for this "stripped book."

To Judy Moran, Lydia Lundberg and Marianne Molle.
Three women who have made their way in a man's world
with style and finesse.

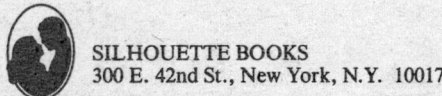

SILHOUETTE BOOKS
300 E. 42nd St., New York, N.Y. 10017

NOBODY'S PERFECT

Copyright © 1992 by Anne Hansen

All rights reserved. Except for use in any review, the reproduction or utilization of this work in whole or in part in any form by any electronic, mechanical or other means, now known or hereafter invented, including xerography, photocopying and recording, or in any information storage or retrieval system, is forbidden without the permission of the publisher, Silhouette Books, 300 E. 42nd St., New York, N.Y. 10017

ISBN: 0-373-08875-2

First Silhouette Books printing July 1992

All the characters in this book have no existence outside the imagination of the author and have no relation whatsoever to anyone bearing the same name or names. They are not even distantly inspired by any individual known or unknown to the author, and all incidents are pure invention.

®: Trademark used under license and registered in the United States Patent and Trademark Office and in other countries.

Printed in the U.S.A.

Books by Anne Peters

Silhouette Romance

Through Thick and Thin #739
Next Stop: Marriage #803
And Daddy Makes Three #821
Storky Jones Is Back in Town #850
Nobody's Perfect #875

Silhouette Desire

Like Wildfire #497

ANNE PETERS

makes her home in the Pacific Northwest with her husband and their dog, Adrienne. Family and friends, reading, writing and travel—those are the things she loves the most. Not always in that order, not always with equal fervor, but always without exception.

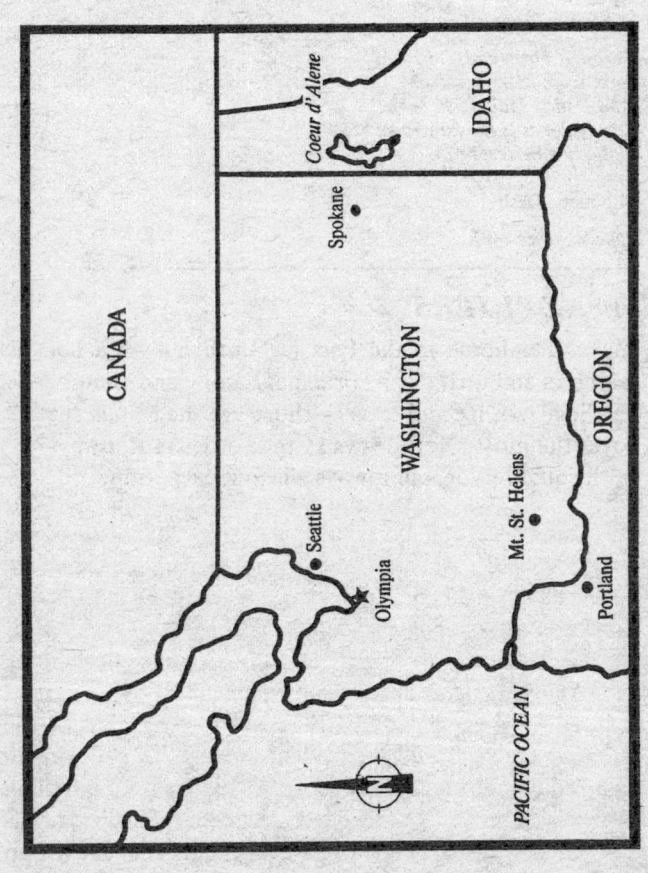

Chapter One

B. J. Rawlings stood by the massive floor-to-ceiling fieldstone fireplace in Floyd Morrison's living room and studied the milling throng of guests with a mixture of curiosity and trepidation. She supposed she ought to mingle, but something—though certainly not the blatant stare of that man across the room—made her reluctant to do so.

Parties like this had never been her style—in fact, she loathed, and usually avoided, attending them. In this instance, however, declining had not been an option.

It was Morrison Erectors' thirtieth anniversary. Floyd Morrison, president and CEO, was justly proud of the success and durability of the business he had single-handedly built into a major force in the material-handling industry. The way he had put it to B.J. in the course of his invitation was, "I mean to have a shindig that'll light up the sky."

As a consequence, scores of business and personal friends, as well as numerous relatives and most of the

Morrison work force filled the rooms of his mansion on the shore of Lake Coeur D'Alene this cold and snowy February night. There was food and drink of every description, a three-piece combo made music that struggled to add a degree of harmony to the unceasing cacophony of muted conversations, and those with good hearing danced. Later on in the evening a fireworks display over the lake was to be the finale.

If it had been any other party, B.J. wouldn't have come. Not because of icy roads and predictions of more snow, though both of those were realities, and not because festivities of this kind bored her, though they did. No, she would have stayed away because her mother's asthma had been particularly bad that day—she had hated to leave her. Her mother had insisted she go, of course, and had been delighted to see her daughter in something slinky and flattering for a change, instead of the customary female version of the corporate gray suit.

"You're a *woman*," she liked to remind her only child, as she had for as far back as B.J. could remember. "You're a *girl*," she used to lament. "I wish just once in a while you and your father would remember that."

Now, surveying the bustling activity in the room before her, B.J. fielded an onslaught of speculative and interested male glances with pretended equanimity. She stifled a sigh. The fact that she was a girl was something *only* she and her father had made it a point to persistently overlook. Everyone else—her attire of shapeless overalls and battered ball caps notwithstanding—had always been dishearteningly quick to take notice of her gender and sometimes even comment on it.

She had been disgusted with her looks all her life, even before she'd metamorphosed from Shirley Temple into Marilyn Monroe. As a small child she had suffered endless attacks of chin chucking, cheek pinching and head patting by adoring adults, strangers or otherwise. Later, people always seemed surprised that she was able to speak in words of more than one syllable.

What really ticked her off, though, was that at age twenty-nine, and in spite of the things she had accomplished, on first impression people *still* took for granted that her flaxen hair and curvaceous *ex*terior masked a dim and vacant *in*terior.

Like that joker with the polished hair and starched suit who'd been ogling her from across the room ever since she walked in, B.J. thought, returning the man's stare with a frosty one of her own.

"Well, B.J.—there you are."

Torn from her reverie by Floyd Morrison's hearty voice, B.J. turned toward his approaching figure with a smile. "Mr. Morrison," she said warmly, extending her hand in greeting.

"Glad to see you made it." Morrison clasped her hand, returning her smile. "And now that you're part of our little family, make that Floyd, why don't you?"

"Why, thank you...Floyd."

"So did you have any trouble finding the place, or with the weather? I forgot you're new around here—" He took her elbow and propelled her away from the fireplace. "I probably should've sent someone by to pick you up."

"Lord, no." B.J. wondered where they were headed with such obvious purpose, and noted that many pairs of eyes were watching their progress. "My car's got four-wheel drive. And Spokane *is* my hometown, after all."

"It is, isn't it? How could I forget?" Morrison grinned down at her. "Memory's the first to go they say, when a body gets old."

The remark was so incongruous, given the man's obvious robust health and legendary, steamroller energy, that B.J. laughed aloud and wordlessly shook her head.

"Have you eaten?" Floyd asked, visibly pleased with her reaction.

"No, I haven't."

"Well, then—" He indicated the heavily laden buffet table just ahead. "What say we put a hole in this together?"

"Something, isn't she?"

"Hmm?" Frowning, Derek Coleman tore his attention away from the woman to whom he'd found his gaze repeatedly drawn, and turned to the man at his elbow.

"I said, the old man's latest playmate's a real stunner," Jack Carruthers restated, adding, "The man's sixty-one years old. How the hell does he do it?"

Derek slanted him a look. "Jealous?"

Jack grinned. "Look, man, I'll admit to being *impressed*, but not to being jealous. Carol'd have my hide."

"And rightly so. Your wife's no slouch herself in the looks department."

"Not to mention that she's got a damn good head on her shoulders."

"If you'd raise your eyes a couple of notches, you'd see that Floyd's playgirl of the month does, too," Derek said dryly.

"Yeah, but what do you wanna bet it's empty?"

"You're probably right." Derek moodily watched as laughter bestowed added sparkle on the blonde's already incandescent features. "On the other hand, judging by old Floyd's silly grin, maybe that's not all bad. See, he's even got her laughing at those corny old jokes of his."

Derek's taste in women had always leaned toward ambitious, intellectual types rather than the run-of-the-mill beauties his buddies seemed to covet. Not that he didn't like to look at a pretty girl as much as the next guy, quite the contrary. It was just that, given a choice, he'd always preferred to spend time with a Plain Jane with brains rather than with a gorgeous mental midget.

Until Margo Swift. She had been both smart *and* beautiful. He'd married her.

Derek grimaced at the recollection, and caught Jack Carruther's mischievous glance. "What?"

"I was thinking that maybe here's your chance to unload some crummy old jokes of your own," Jack told him. "Might cheer you up to run a few of 'em past yonder lady...."

Derek's glare was quelling. "You seem to forget who signs your expense vouchers, pal."

"Only until the new district manager arrives," Jack blithely pointed out. "By the way, when *is* that?"

"Monday, last I heard." Derek made the reply absently, his eyes once again on the blonde. Floyd had escorted her to a couple of the company's middle managers and their wives, made some introductions and then left her there with them. It was interesting to watch the expressions on the men's faces—a mixture of delight and trepidation. The latter no doubt in response to their wives' undisguised reserve toward, not to say disapproval of, Floyd's sexy siren.

She was making a valiant attempt at conversation, her smile friendly, but when she inadvertently cast a helpless glance in his general direction, Derek, without conscious decision, abruptly picked up one of Jack's hands and closed its fingers around his empty glass.

"Think I'll go rescue a damsel in distress," he said, and left Jack standing there with a glass in each hand and his mouth open.

Derek nodded to people here and there as he purposefully strode the length of the living room. He stepped through the wide, arched opening which separated the living and dining room just as the blonde was taking her leave from the group on which Floyd Morrison had foisted her. Rather than head toward the living room—and him—however, she turned toward the door leading out into the hall.

Derek passed and intercepted her in three long strides.

"Hel-*lo*," he said, aware of being avidly observed by the four people the woman in front of him had just left. Lord, but she was appealing up close. Huge sky blue eyes ringed by impossibly long, dark lashes met his gaze, and even though the expression in those eyes was at the moment far from friendly, he found himself wanting to drown in their sparkling depths.

"Not leaving already?" His voice sounded rusty, his mouth had suddenly gone desert dry and his pulses leaped in a—for him—totally uncharacteristic reaction. He'd felt unadulterated lust before, but nothing quite like this. This was different. This was... scary.

And this was another man's—his *boss's*—woman, he reminded himself, drawing a deep breath which didn't calm him in the least. "You'll miss the fireworks."

"Excuse me." If she didn't get out of here, B.J. thought grimly, in just another second she would *be* the fireworks. She tried to step around the stuffed shirt whose steady gaze had been at her like pinpricks all night, and who was eyeing her now like his favorite dessert, but he was squarely in her path. Ordinarily she might have been amused about this—heaven knew she'd endured more than her share of similar looks and pickup approaches—but thanks to the frostbite she'd just suffered in the company of those self-righteous biddies and their spineless spouses, she was all out of tolerance. "Let me pass."

"I beg your pardon." The man moved aside, but to B.J.'s intense annoyance fell into step beside her. "I'm Derek Coleman," he introduced himself when they were out in the hall.

The name gave B.J. pause. Eyes wide, she turned to him. "Derek P. Coleman?" Coleman was Morrison's national sales manager—Floyd had spoken highly of him.

"None other." He smiled, and B.J. was astounded by the change that smile brought to his face. Gone were the harsh, almost forbidding lines, the look of cynicism which had put her off even from across the room. Smiling, he appeared young, even boyish, and in spite of the ruthlessly slicked-back hair and ultra-staid suit, he was unsettlingly attractive.

"How do you do," she said, warming in response to that smile as she extended her hand to him. "I'm—"

"I know, Floyd's friend." Derek found himself wanting to spare this lovely young thing any potential awkwardness. He took the hand she held out to him. It felt soft and fragile in his, and caused a surge of protectiveness none of the other always-so-capable women in his past had ever elicited. He found he enjoyed the feeling, primitive though it was. It made a man feel... well, like a *man*. Invincible. In charge.

Insufferable, Margo would have said, because she had spent every waking moment of their marriage trying to prove to him that she was, at the very least, any man's equal.

Derek banished her from his mind, grateful that here was a woman who he'd bet had no such aspirations. "I wonder, would you care to dance?"

"Dance?" B.J. was still puzzled over something Coleman had said just prior to his invitation. What had he meant, referring to her as Floyd's *friend* with such peculiar emphasis? She and Morrison were virtual strangers. Including their initial meeting at that trade show in Denver two years ago, and not counting tonight, she had met with the man a sum total of three times, though they had corresponded. At a loss, she hedged, "Well, I..."

"Floyd won't mind, if that's what's bothering you," Derek assured her, though with more optimism than conviction, and for the simple reason that he wanted to feel this sexy woman in his arms. It was crazy. *He* was crazy, all the more so because he was thinking he'd like to take her away from Morrison and make her his.

Since the breakup of his marriage three years ago, he had avoided entanglements, avoided women. *All* women. Now he knew he'd been a fool, because here was proof that there were still women out there—soft, warm, beautiful but simple women—whose ambitions were limited to making a man happy.

How did he know the woman in front of him was one of those?

Derek smiled at the question. It was so obvious. She exuded warmth and sensuality—her body in the slinky little cocktail thing she wore was lush, made for love. Her face was that of an angel: innocent, open, with eyes that held an expression of such bewildered wonder, it tugged at his heart.

Bless her, he thought indulgently, she didn't know what was happening. But he knew. Oh, yes—he knew. He looked at her mouth, traced with his eyes the soft, full lower lip and short, sweetly curved upper. They were slightly parted, those lips...

Derek had to shut his eyes and drag in a deep breath to steady his pulse. He wanted to kiss her.

When he looked at her again, he caught her frowning. Without thinking, he raised a hand to smooth her brow. "Don't," he murmured, not wanting to see her perfection marred.

B.J. felt the touch of Derek Coleman's fingers like a caress and had to force herself not to flinch. This was the craziest encounter she had ever experienced, bar none. It was as if they were talking on two distinctly separate levels here.

And then a light bulb clicked on in her head.

"Good *Lord,*" she exclaimed, at once shocked, dismayed and tickled by the sheer lunacy of the revelation she'd just had: Derek Coleman thought she was Floyd Morrison's...

No, it was too much. Staring at him, B.J. clapped a hand over her mouth and gave in to a fit of helpless laughter. "Mr. Coleman," she gasped, when finally she could speak. "I'm afraid you misunderstand. You see, Floyd and I—"

"No." Derek Coleman laid a finger across her lips and silenced her. "Right now I don't care about Floyd and you. He's not here, but I am. And I'd very much like to dance with you."

His words and actions dispelled any doubts B.J. might have had about the veracity of her assumption. Ordinarily she would have taken umbrage, would have set the man straight and turned him off with a few well-chosen words, but for some reason just then she felt another bubble of mirth threaten to erupt. And something else, something mischievous, devilish and reckless, the likes of which she rarely, if ever, permitted expression.

It was foolishness—it could well mean trouble. But somehow, at least for that moment, B.J. couldn't bring herself to give a damn.

She pursed her lips ever so slightly against Derek's silencing finger, and though he instantly withdrew it, she knew from the flicker of gold in his hazel brown eyes that he had felt the subtle caress.

"All right," she purred, doing her best to emphasize the naturally husky quality of her voice. "If you're sure Floyd won't mind..."

"I'm sure." His hand low on her back, Derek guided her up the hall and into a room at the other side of the spacious front entry. The room's dark paneled walls were book lined, proclaiming it as den or library, but whatever furniture it might have held had been removed, leaving its hardwood floor clear for dancing. The small band in the living room across the entry was doing its thing loud enough for the dancers to hear and follow the slow, pulsing rhythms.

Only a few other couples, none of whom Derek recognized, were in the room. In response to the pressure of Derek's hand on her back, B.J. turned to face him. For the length of a heartbeat their gazes met, and it seemed time was suspended as they looked at each other.

The craziest feelings and notions took possession of B.J.—thoughts of satin sheets and hot kisses, and longings for... more. Startled, and not just a little shocked by these inappropriate and unwelcome reactions, she blinked, and when Derek put one arm around her while his other hand clasped hers and led her into the dance, she prayed he wouldn't notice her racing pulse.

She smiled at him, but it was a strained effort, at best. "N-nice party, isn't it?" she murmured, inwardly wincing at the inanity which, she could see, amused Derek Coleman. No doubt she'd just confirmed his assessment of her limited mental capacity.

"Very nice," he said, and B.J. was appalled to see him give her exactly the kind of smile those chin chuckers and cheek pinchers had used to bestow on her as a little girl. Indulgent, even tender. This charade had not been a good idea.

"Do you know how sweet you are?" he added softly.

Softly and rhetorically, B.J. thought, her teeth on edge. Were there women who actually enjoyed these witless platitudes?

His lips now grazed her temple. "What's your name, honey?"

Honey. Everything in her demanded she kick the man's shin. Her little joke was fast wearing thin.

"Joanie," she breathed against his throat, and longed to take a bite out of it. Instead, though, she leaned away and fluttered her lashes. "Do you like it?"

"It suits you. What is it you do, Joanie?"

"Do?" B.J. blinked in consternation. Now, what should she reply to *that* question?

"When you're not attending parties and driving men crazy, that is," Derek elaborated teasingly, but with such an unmistakable gleam in his eyes that B.J. knew, irrevocably, that in getting herself into this she had gravely erred.

"Look, Mr. Coleman—" She was desperate now to call a halt to her charade.

"Derek."

"No." B.J.'s tone grew more urgent. "Mr. Coleman, please, I must tell you—"

"Derek, can I see you a minute?" Floyd Morrison stood in the doorway, beckoning with his hand when Derek looked toward him.

The Old Man didn't appear to be upset at catching him dancing with Joanie, Derek thought. On the other hand, the man was sophisticated enough not to let it show if he did care.

"Excuse me, Joanie, would you?" If there was to be a confrontation, he might as well get it over with. "Don't go away."

Oh, brother. Watching Morrison clasp Derek Coleman's shoulders as the two of them walked off, B.J.'s sigh came up from out of her toes somewhere. This was awful. How was she going to explain to the man that she'd only been trying to be funny? He didn't look like a man with much of a sense of humor.

Damn. Thoroughly put out with herself, B.J. left the room, only to bump smack into Floyd Morrison himself. B.J. saw at a glance that Derek was not with him, and felt a most peculiar mixture of relief and disappointment. Lord, but she was feeling weird tonight, she thought.

"Ah." Morrison steadied her. "Just the woman I was looking for. Coleman's out there supervising the fireworks. Join me in watching them, won't you?"

B.J. briefly weighed the risks of refusing against the risks of sticking around and getting herself into even bigger trouble. She decided the safest place for her was home.

"Mr. Morrison—"

"Floyd."

"Floyd. Would you mind terribly if I left? It's been a lovely evening, but my mother hasn't been feeling very well lately, and it's quite a drive back to Spokane...."

"Say no more." Floyd held up his hand. "You go right on home, young lady, and take care of your mother. You got a wrap somewhere?"

"In the cloakroom. But I can get it, thank you."

"Can you see yourself out, too?"

"You bet."

"All right, then." Morrison gave her a nod. "I'll see you Monday morning."

B.J. was glad she had left the party when she did. By the time she pulled into the carport next to her mother's small house, it was snowing and blowing hard. Even with four-wheel drive and her considerable experience with winter driving, a whiteout was something in which she would rather not be caught.

Even if it had been a balmy summer's eve, though, she would still have been glad to be home. Apart from being genuinely concerned about her mother's condition, she knew she would not have been up to another tête-à-tête with Derek Coleman. She owed the man an explanation for her behavior—actually, he owed her at least the same—but since he was who he was, and the situation being what *it* was, B.J. knew the utmost in tact and diplomacy on her part would be called for. Given the odd way she'd been feeling tonight, she just knew she would have blown it if she'd stayed.

She stomped her booted feet to rid them of snow—her dress shoes were in her coat pockets—and let herself into the enclosed porch fronting the house. In the summer there were screens in front of the wide porch windows and wicker chairs on which to sit and gaze out at the neighbors. Now, however, lacy frost designs rendered those windows opaque, and the only difference between being out in the elements and being inside this porch was that it didn't snow and blow in here.

B.J. tugged off her boots and quickly hobbled the few steps to the inner front door with toes curled up and away from the cold wooden floor. The hinges squeaked as she opened the door, reminding her that she had wanted to oil them earlier and had forgotten. Lots of things around the house had gone to pot in the years she had been away; it was a good thing she was fairly handy with tools.

Meanwhile she hoped the noise hadn't awakened her mother, but the soft, slightly wheezy call of her name told her it had.

"Yes, it's me, Mom," she called back, letting the door fall shut behind her. She peered into the room immediately to her right, the living room. "You in here?"

"Yes, darling."

"Why are you sitting in the dark, for heaven's sake?" B.J. walked farther into the room and fumbled for the switch on the swag lamp in the corner. After her father had died seven years earlier, her mother had sat like this night after night for months. In the dark, grieving. It had been terrible for B.J. to watch this grief, and for a while she had been terrified that her mother would become lost to her, too.

In the muted light from the lamp she had just turned on, B.J. saw that Bertie was sitting in her favorite chair by the fireplace. The fire B.J. had started before leaving for the party was only a glimmer now.

She rushed over to her mother, and kneeling in front of her, took her hands and chafed them between both of hers. "Your hands are cold," she scowled lovingly, scanning her mother's tired face without betraying the worry she felt. "Why are you still up? It's nearly midnight."

"That's not so late." Smiling, Bertie leaned forward and kissed her daughter's forehead. "In fact, it's darn early to be coming home from a party. Didn't you enjoy yourself?"

"It was lovely." Because her mother so rarely got out these days, and because B.J. knew how much she'd always loved dinner parties and such, she described in great detail the beautiful rooms, the scrumptious buffet, the elegant dresses. "They were just about to start a fireworks display when I left," she concluded. "But the way the weather is turning out..." She shrugged.

"Is that why you didn't stay and watch?" her mother exclaimed. "Or did you leave because of me? Darling, I don't want you worrying so. You promised you wouldn't...."

"I didn't," B.J. fibbed, though the truth was she worried constantly. She had left a great job in Denver because of that worry; she had no longer been able to bear the thought of her mother sick and alone. Lonely. Bertie was only fifty-four years old; she had a life yet to live. B.J. wanted her to live it, to have fun, to go places. Places such as Arizona in the winter and Alaska on a cruise ship in the summer, if she chose.

Floyd Morrison had promised B.J. the opportunity to make a lot of money, as well as the chance to relocate to Spokane. It had been an offer she had, all things considered, not been able to refuse. Truth to tell, she'd been looking forward to the new challenge, but now, after the fiasco with Derek Coleman...

"Was everyone nice?" her mother was asking.

B.J. thought of the biddies and grimaced. But all she said was, "Actually, I didn't meet very many people. You know how these things are, Mom—everyone clustered in little groups." She pulled another face. "I'm not very good at just planting myself next to people and joining their conversation."

"But that's *exactly* what you're supposed to do, child. That's what everyone does."

"Well, whenever I do it, people seem to fall silent and give me this look that says, 'Butt out.'"

"Nonsense," her mother said flatly. "You're not socially inept. You wouldn't have gotten where you are, if you were."

B.J. wearily got to her feet. "I didn't get where I am by rubbing elbows at cocktail parties, Mom, but by hard work. Hard work, along with the brains you and Pop were good enough to pass on to me, the education he insisted I get, and my own stubborn determination to show Pop I could do it."

Aware that in the course of her reply she'd gone tense with emotion, and that she had balled her hands into fists, B.J. let out a long breath while slanting her mother a rueful grin. "See how intense I get? That's what got me there."

She held out her hand, and when Bertie gripped it, gently pulled her mother to her feet. "Come on, let's go to bed."

She made to turn, but her mother laid a hand on B.J.'s cheek and stayed her. "You're a wonderful daughter, B. J. Rawlings," she said softly. Since B.J., at five foot seven, was a good five inches taller, she raised herself on tiptoe and pressed a sweet kiss on her daughter's lips.

"Pop used to say with just a little more effort I'd make a pretty good son," B.J. recalled, giving Bertie an affectionate squeeze.

Her mother's eyes dimmed. "Yes, well—your father and I didn't always see things the same way where you were concerned."

"Remind me to oil the front door tomorrow, will you?" B.J. clicked off the light and led the way out of the room. "And to check the pipes and outside faucets to make sure they don't freeze."

"Aye aye, sir."

They chuckled, and then Bertie said, "I'm so glad you're home again, darling."

Beneath her nearly ankle-length fleece-lined raincoat, B.J. had dressed with care. She had chosen her most conservative, severely tailored suit, her crispest blouse and her most muted scarf, which she had fashioned into something resembling a tie. Her shoulder-length hair was swept back from her face and caught at the base of her skull by a wide tortoiseshell clasp. Cultured pearl studs adorned her earlobes and her grandmother's engagement ring was on the ring finger of her right hand as it always was. She wore no other jewelry.

Pulling into the parking lot in front of the Morrison Erectors facility—a sprawling, single-story office building, a huge yard and several large, hangar-like buildings B.J. knew to be the various manufacturing shops—she tried to recall which numbered stall Floyd Morrison had said would be hers.

She was early—it was barely seven o'clock in the morning—and though the shop was clearly already in full operation, the lot in front of the office building was as yet all but deserted. The official workday wouldn't start for another hour.

Slowly she drove up one aisle and then down the one that was closest to the building. A couple of the stalls there were occupied, one by a stately silver gray Mercedes she knew belonged to Morrison himself. Noting that the vacant ones had the designated occupant's title painted along the top, she saw that the national sales manager had not yet arrived. Relieved, she pulled into the adjacent slot which bore her own job title.

A security person sat at a desk just inside the building's front door. B.J. gave him her name, which he verified against a list on his clipboard before giving her directions to the executive offices. On the way there, she shed her coat.

The door to Floyd Morrison's office was ajar—B.J. could hear him talking to another man. Shifting her briefcase to her left hand, she knocked. "Good morning..."

"Come in, come in."

As B.J. pushed the door farther open, someone was likewise pulling it from the inside. A small, slender man of middle age, B.J. discovered, exchanging polite smiles with him as she entered.

Floyd was seated behind a massive mahogany desk, but rose as she approached. "You're early," he said. "I like that."

"Well, I thought I'd have a chance to nose around a bit, get my bearings."

B.J. turned as Floyd gestured toward the other man. "Meet Henry Smith, our personnel manager. Hank, B. J. Rawlings."

"Mr. Smith."

"Call me Hank."

They shook hands. "And I'm B.J."

"Right." He cleared his throat. "If you like, and if it's all right with you, Floyd, maybe we should get the paperwork out of the way before the others get here for the staff meeting."

"Good idea," Floyd said. "B.J.? Any objections?"

"No, that's fine. Great." She followed Smith out the door.

The session in personnel was strictly a matter of taking care of the legalities: taxes, social security and the like. B.J.'s contract, benefits, salary and incentive plan had long since been put to paper by B.J. and Floyd Morrison in the course of their negotiations following his offer of employment.

After she had signed the last form and her picture had been taken for the security badge she would be issued, B.J. walked with Hank Smith toward the conference room where the weekly staff meetings were held.

Floyd met them at the door. "Everyone's already inside," he said, "so we might as well go in, too."

B.J. didn't know who "everyone" was, of course, but she did know Derek P. Coleman would be one of their number. Suddenly her heart was racing, fueled by an equal mix of anticipation and trepidation. She had to swallow and firmly remind herself that she was a professional about to meet her peers, not a silly schoolgirl coming face-to-face with some adored matinee idol.

Head high, she preceded Hank Smith and Floyd Morrison into the room.

Chapter Two

The very last person Derek would have expected to see walk into the Monday morning staff meeting at Morrison Erectors was Joanie, the latest and most gorgeous of Floyd Morrison's legendary string of luscious Lolitas. Yet that was precisely who did walk in.

Chin up, bold as brass, cool as a cucumber. And still just as sexy as sin.

Someone had dressed her up to resemble high fashion's version of an investment banker and had tortured her hair into the severe style worn by flamenco dancers—minus the curlicue commas. Who? And how dared they?

Half out of his seat, propelled as much by some undefined sense of outrage as by whatever emotion it was that had kept her on his mind for the entire weekend, Derek caught sight of Floyd Morrison's bulky form in the doorway. Jaws clenched, he subsided back into his chair.

Old Floyd had dared, of course. He'd probably made the woman a secretary or an assistant or something, in order to keep her handy. Derek despised the man for stooping to such tawdry shenanigans, but right at the moment there wasn't a hell of a lot he could do about it.

Grimly he stared at Joanie. He'd asked her what she did, and now he knew. She did whatever Floyd wanted her to do.

Something curdled in Derek's stomach, putting a sour taste in his mouth. He'd thought she was sweet, different. Not as pure and untouched as she seemed, of course—he might be a fool, but he wasn't naive. Without a doubt she'd been around the block a time or two—after all she was even now "going with" a man who was more than old enough to be her father, and sure as hell not for true love. He could handle that—after all, his own motives were similarly uncomplicated. He wanted Joanie in his arms, in his bed, as soon as possible and for as long as it was fun for them both.

Right now, though, all he wanted was to get up and slam his fist into a wall or, better yet, into Floyd Morrison's ample midsection.

"Gentlemen." Floyd called the meeting to order. "Before we get down to regular business, I'd like to introduce a new member on our team. Our new district sales manager, B. J. Rawlings."

As Floyd proceeded to introduce the half dozen men around the table, each of whom in turn nodded and murmured hellos, Derek sat thunderstruck.

This was the district sales manager Morrison had been so smugly secretive about? This was the *ace* the Old Man claimed to have enticed away from H. E. Young and Co. of Denver, Colorado, and at considerable cost?

The curdling in his stomach intensified as he forced his attention back to the proceedings at hand.

"... and last, but definitely not least," Morrison was saying to B.J., "we have Derek Coleman, the man whose praises I've sung to you in the course of our negotiations, and whose personal acquaintance you made at the party on Saturday night. If you work together as well as the two of you danced together, I believe we can expect great things for Morrison Erectors."

As everyone duly chuckled and a few applauded, it struck Derek with all the impact of a sledgehammer's blow to the back of his head that Joanie—B. J. Rawlings, he bitterly corrected himself—had purposely misled him on Saturday might. She had made a fool of him, laughed at him.

The look Derek gave her as she dutifully shook his hand made B.J. want to run. Which is why she stiffened her knees and spine and kept her own gaze perfectly level.

"Actually," she said evenly, "Mr. Coleman and I weren't formally introduced—"

"But when I told you my name, you knew who I was, didn't you?" Derek interrupted coldly, his forbidding expression daring her to deny it.

There was no way she would. "Yes," she said. "I knew."

Derek's only response was a thinning of the lips.

"Well." Morrison rubbed his hands and beamed at the assembled group. "I believe I speak for all of us when I say to our new district sales manager, 'Welcome aboard.'" He turned to B.J. "Would you like to say a few words before you sit down?"

"Thank you. Yes, I would." Drawing herself up to her not inconsiderable height, B.J. let her eyes rest briefly on every masculine face turned toward her. Knowing only too well now the folly of relying on first, superficial impressions, she tried not to judge or interpret the expressions her gaze encountered, nor to be daunted by the forbidding one Derek Coleman wore. She would straighten things out with him later, in private.

"All I really want to say," she began, "is that I'm happy to be back in Spokane, where I grew up, and that I look forward to the challenges ahead. I believe that Morrison Erectors builds a product we can all be proud of, and it will be my privilege and distinct honor to be part of the team that markets it.

"I won't bore you with the details of my experience in the field of industrial sales, nor will I cite a long list of academic credentials. Suffice it to say that Mr. Morrison—" the smile she slanted toward the CEO made the fine hairs at the back of Derek's neck bristle "—that *Floyd*," B.J. corrected with an inclination of her head, "considered them sufficiently adequate. They got me the job," she said, grinning at each of the men now in a way that made every one of them preen and made Derek gnash his teeth. "But I know it'll be my performance *on* the job that will convince you that I not only deserve to *have* it, but that I also deserve to *keep* it. We'll talk again in three months. Thank you for your attention."

Both B.J. and Derek hoped for extensive minutes of the meeting that followed, because neither grasped more than the gist of it.

Though not for the same reasons.

B.J., because the confrontation she knew she would have to have with Derek Coleman hung above her head like the sword of Damocles and she couldn't relax.

Derek, because he felt so betrayed, humiliated and furious that throughout the entire meeting it was all he could do not to turn his body forty-five degrees toward the Rawlings woman, lift his hands and strangle her.

And now they were across the desk from each other in his office.

Derek was seated, but he had not invited B.J. to do the same. He'd show her who was boss, he fumed, brushing aside the niggling voice which told him he was acting like a petulant child. She'd tried to make a fool of him; she'd no doubt laughed at him, well—they'd see which of them was still laughing a few weeks down the road.

His motions brisk, he opened her personnel file. It didn't contain many sheets of paper. Her academic record: BSc, Mechanical engineering, Washington State University, Pullman. Honors. Dean's list.

He shot her a look.

She offered a smile. Tentatively.

He frowned. Probably cheated on her exams, or more likely got some guy to take 'em for her. Even as he thought it, Derek knew he was way off base and none of that could have been possible, but it suited his mood to imagine awful and outrageous things about her.

His gaze returned to her file. MBA, University of Washington, Seattle. Honors.

He clenched his jaw and forbade himself to look up. She was expecting him to, he'd bet on it. She was waiting to see him stare at her in awe. "Why, Ms. Rawlings," she no doubt expected him to intone, "you're brilliant as well as beautiful. Lucky us."

She was expecting him to be impressed. Anyone else probably would be. Floyd clearly had been. Derek flipped the page and skimmed the one below. Highest sales at H. E. Young & Co. two years in a row; a couple of patents—not on anything earthshaking, but innovations that made the product more saleable.

She was a thinker, Derek realized, no doubt about it. A mover and shaker. The kind of hotshot he'd be thrilled to death to have on his team—if that hotshot were a man.

No. Derek leaned back in his chair, closing his eyes and pinching the bridge of his nose between thumb and middle finger. Not just a man. Anybody else, any other woman but this one particular woman who had charmed and bewitched him on Saturday night, and who he had thought was different.

It hurt—yes, he could admit to that now—it hurt like hell to have her turn out to be of the same ilk as every other woman he had ever been drawn to. To have her be just like Margo.

He opened his eyes when he heard her discreetly clear her throat. He gazed at her balefully. "Yes?"

"Are you feeling all right?" Genuine concern clouded her beautiful eyes. "Can I get you some aspirin?"

"I'm fine." Squaring his shoulders, he glanced down again at her file.

"Bertha Joanne Rawlings," he read aloud, brows rising sharply when she interrupted with a comically dismayed, "B.J., *please!*"

One brow arched. "You're sure it's not Joanie?"

B.J. flushed. "Look," she began in a conciliatory tone, "about Saturday night—"

"Forget Saturday night," Derek interrupted, jumping to his feet and leaning across the desk as if to physically launch himself across it. "And you look. Whatever you might have thought was happening wasn't, do you understand me?"

"Perfectly," B.J. said with dignity.

His gaze narrowed on hers, and they studied one another in silence for several charged moments. At length, Derek sat down. Shrugging his shoulders as if he suddenly found his perfectly cut charcoal gray suit jacket somehow confining, he cleared his throat and stared at the top sheet in her file. The one bearing her name. Her full name.

Bertha Joanne Rawlings.

Always, and to this day, B.J. shuddered at the knowledge that this was what she was called. She didn't mind the Joanne. It was her grandmother's name. Her *Rawlings* grandmother's name.

It was the name Bertha she couldn't abide. She would have changed it long ago, but the one and only time she had mentioned this, her mother had burst into tears.

"You can't," she had wailed. "Don't you know it's not done?"

B.J. had told her it was done all the time. That people all over the world changed their names, some of them more frequently than they changed their underwear.

Her mother had not been amused. "*My* name is Bertha," she had told her daughter, as if that should make it all right, "but everyone calls me Bertie." She had brightened. "Would you like us to call you Bertie, too?"

To B.J., Bertie Two seemed no better than Bertha and she had said as much to her mother who had looked saddened.

"*My* mother—your Grandmother Ellis—was also called Bertha, and her mother before that. And all the first daughters in the family before that," Bertie had said, "all the way back to the Anguses who came across from Scotland right after the *Mayflower*..."

It was at that point that B.J. had surrendered her plans for a formal name change, recognizing with a heavy heart that there were simply some traditions with which one didn't willy-nilly tamper. She had contented herself with forbidding anyone to address her by anything but her initials.

Now, waiting for Derek Coleman to look up, B.J. silently dared him to make just one more crack about it. She'd let him have it, then. She would *really* let him have it. The nerve of him, anyway, keeping her standing in front of his desk like some recalcitrant schoolgirl who'd been called to the principal.

Who did he think she was? For that matter, who did he think *he* was? Sure, he was her superior—strictly speaking and corporate ladder-wise. But not in a hiring/firing way; and not in a you'd-better-do-as-I-say way.

Chin up, B.J. sat down.

Derek looked up.

B.J. offered another smile. A small one, and just to show she was willing to meet him halfway.

Derek frowned and snapped her file shut. "Ms. Rawlings—"

"B.J." She allowed her smile to sweeten.

Derek's frown darkened. "Ms. Rawlings," he repeated with emphasis, looking down at his hands and clearing his throat when her smile faded, "our positions here at Morrison Erectors require us to work closely together from time to time. How closely will, of course, depend on the particular project you're working on, the circumstances, and so forth..."

"I understand."

At her level tone, he glanced up. He told himself he was glad she looked as composed and unemotional now as he hoped he did. Earlier, he'd felt like a heel when his brusqueness had caused her smile to flee.

"We are both of us professionals," he went on, stalwartly refusing to acknowledge the flash of regret he felt because "Joanie" had merely been an illusion, wishful thinking on his part. How could he have forgotten that careers were the thing for the woman of today, and husbands, *families,* go hang. "I trust we can do the job we've been hired to do without letting personalities intrude."

"Absolutely."

"Fine." He rose, and so did B.J. "I'll show you to your office and introduce you to your secretary." He was halfway out the door before she had retrieved her briefcase from the floor beside her chair. "And I'll send some files and lists of active prospects for you to study," he tossed back across one shoulder. Without waiting to see if she followed, he marched down the hall, then stopped by a door, and with ingrained and automatic courtesy held it while B.J. preceded him inside. Catching a whiff of her scent as she swept past him, Derek's nostrils flared. He stifled an oath.

The job he loved was going to be hell from now on.

B.J. decided she and Cally James, her secretary, were going to get along great. Cally was twenty-one, a whiz with modem and mouse, and thoroughly independent. Give her a stack of diskettes, files or memos, and she took it from there, leaving B.J. relatively unencumbered of the routine paperwork she despised.

B.J. liked to sell, to be in front of a prospect and demonstrate to him or her the myriad ways her product would save him money, production time and maintenance headaches. She thrived on the give-and-take, the feint-and-parry of these high-stakes negotiations where, as often as not, millions of dollars were involved. She loved the challenge of outwitting the competition and thoroughly enjoyed the cloak-and-dagger methods with which each competitor tried to ferret out the other's prices.

She also loved to succeed, but never more than right now. And all because of Derek Coleman. She would show him the stuff she was made of, she vowed, or kill herself trying.

For over a week now she had studied every Morrison Erectors catalogue, parts list and sample spec she could get her hands on, until she knew them by heart. Letters of introduction had been sent out into the industry and she had familiarized herself with the active prospects in her territory, which encompassed the states of Idaho and Oregon, as well as Washington. She was ready to get to work.

A couple of very lively prospects were located west of the Cascades in the Seattle area, it seemed to B.J., flipping through a stack of reports. Had one of Morrison's salesmen made contact? Was Morrison on the bidders' lists? She needed some answers.

She picked up the phone and stabbed the single digit which was the speed-dial number for Derek Coleman's office. Except for the weekly staff meeting, she had only seen him in passing and had talked to him on the phone only once. He had told her then to make a written list of the questions for which she sought answers and have her secretary submit them to Muriel Cooper, who was *his* secretary.

Great. Fine and dandy. B.J. grimaced. Today, though, only verbal communication would do.

"B. J. Rawlings," she said when Muriel answered. "Is Mr. Coleman free?"

"Let me check."

B.J. waited, drumming her fingers, silently daring him to refuse to take her call. She'd march right over there and collar him personally, and remind him of what he himself had said: they were professionals, dammit....

"Coleman."

"Oh, uh, hello." Caught off guard in the midst of her mental harangue, B.J.'s fingers abruptly stilled. "I..." Damn, she was completely rattled. She tried again. "I—"

"Ms. Rawlings," Derek Coleman said briskly, "I can only spare you about three minutes. I suggest you either organize your thoughts and call me back, or, better still, put them in writing." Click.

He'd hung up! Slack jawed with shock, B.J. slowly pulled the receiver away from her ear and stared at it. Just like that, the man had hung up.

Fury unlike any she'd ever experienced erupted. Leaping to her feet, she slammed down the phone and was out the door before she'd formulated even one coherent thought beyond, How dare he?

She flew on winged feet past a startled Cally, marched three doors up the hall and past a wide-eyed Muriel who spun around on her swivel chair and was half out of it when B.J. gave an abbreviated rap on Coleman's door and sailed through.

Derek had been sitting and moodily staring at the phone he had just hung up, feeling none too proud of himself, when his door all but flew off its hinges and the subject of his dour thoughts entered like one of the very furies themselves.

Too startled to do more than stare in astonishment and—yes, dammit—grudging admiration, Derek watched B.J. plant her fists on his desk while her eyes spat blue flames.

"Don't you ever," she enunciated through clenched teeth, "*ever* do that to me again."

"Now look just a minute—" Derek began, only to be cut off.

"I'm not finished, Mr. Coleman." B.J. straightened. Chin high, she regarded him down her small, tip-tilted nose. "I am not some flunky you can jerk around, so either you get your act together and shake off that chip on your shoulder so that we can get on with the job we were *both* hired to do, or we can go to Floyd Morrison right now and you can explain to *him* what your problem is."

"I don't have a problem—"

"Oh, yes, you do."

"—and there's no need to bother your sugar daddy..."

"What?!!"

"Oh, *damn!*" Knowing he'd gone too far, and feeling like dirt in the face of B.J.'s red-faced incredulity, Derek leaped to his feet. "God, I'm sorry. Please forgive me."

He made to touch her shoulder but she jerked away, staring at him as if he'd just crawled out from under some rock. "That was despicable."

"I agree." Derek would have preferred to look anywhere but into those outraged pansy eyes of hers. He couldn't believe he had said what he had; couldn't imagine what had possessed him. Even if it were true, though in the face of B.J.'s reaction he no longer believed it, but even if she and the old man *were*...lovers—the thought brought nausea to his stomach—what right did he have to throw it up to her? No right at all. None.

"Please forgive me," he said again.

She regarded him in silence for quite some time before Derek saw bewilderment begin to smooth some of the turbulence in her gaze. "Why?" she finally whispered.

Scowling, Derek tightly compressed his lips as he slowly, wordlessly, shook his head. What could he say that wouldn't sound like a lame excuse or make her feel worse?

"You don't even know me," B.J. persisted. "You know nothing about me except what you read in my file. Why would you say... why would you *think* something so reprehensible...?"

Derek heaved a deep sigh and went back to his chair. "Because I'm a jerk, I s'pose," he said heavily.

"No, you're not," she said flatly. "That's a cop-out, and you know it. Look, Mr. Coleman—" she approached his desk "—if we're going to have any chance at all of working together, I think we'd better clear the air right now. Total honesty. If you like, I'll start."

Derek was completely adrift by now. He had never before met a woman who, when she'd been wronged, didn't milk the situation for all it was worth. It looked as if this woman wasn't going to do that, and he was at a loss as to how to respond, except to say, "All right."

"I'll sit, if you don't mind."

She sat before he even had a chance to say yea or nay. "I'm sorry if by my misrepresentation of myself the night of the party I offended you." She tossed him a self-conscious half smile. "I'd caught you watching me a time or two and I'd gotten the impression that you—" she faltered, a flush rising up from her neck. "You see, men have always had a way of, you know, reacting to my, my looks that I—well, frankly, that I find offensive and demeaning." She looked down at her hands, took a deep breath and raised her gaze back to his. "I thought you were looking at me like *that*."

"I was," he admitted quietly.

"Well." B.J. looked startled, then gave a little laugh. "I wanted honesty and I guess I got it, huh?"

"Yeah." Derek's grin was crooked, self-deprecatory. "I guess I flunked Diplomacy 101."

"I doubt that. You'd hardly be in sales, if you had."

Derek stared at B.J. with something close to wonder. "You really aren't angry anymore, are you?"

"Well, no." She seemed surprised by the question. "Should I be?"

"I don't know," Derek said slowly. "Other women would be."

"Would they? Well." Primly she smoothed her skirt. "I think you'll find I'm not *like* other women."

After two days of sitting in on B.J.'s meetings with prospective customers in Seattle, Derek was beginning to think she might be right. While she wasn't the sexy and sweet airhead he had—chauvinistically, he supposed—taken her to be on first acquaintance, neither was B. J. Rawlings anything like any other woman he had been close to in his time.

She was every bit as intelligent as they, to say the least. And to say she was as beautiful would be an understatement. She was as ambitious, to be sure, and every bit as single-minded, even *driven*—on the job, at least—as, for instance, Margo had been.

Yet there was something about Bertha Joanne Rawlings that set her apart.

Derek didn't know what it was, nor did he quite trust that it was real, but he supposed time would tell. Time and proximity. After all, nothing could better bring out the worst in a person than the pressures and stresses of closing a crucial deal—or losing it. Given the two projects they had been working on these past couple of days, those stresses and pressures would make themselves felt in due course. Until they did, and until he saw how she reacted, he would reserve judgment on the inimitable Ms. Rawlings's character.

She had a lead foot, of that much Derek *was* sure.

It was Saturday morning and they were headed back

from Seattle to Spokane. Originally they had meant to return the night before, but they'd been out with one of the clients and his wife and afterward both he and B.J. had been bushed.

Derek shifted in his seat, trying to catch a glimpse of the speedometer without being obvious about it.

"Sixty," B.J. said, not taking her eyes off the road.

"Speed limit's fifty-five." The woman had eyes at the side of her head, he'd swear.

"Just keeping up with traffic." She switched lanes and passed a van on the right.

"Left lane's the passing lane."

"It was occupied."

Derek sat up straighter, checking his seat belt as she overtook another car and this one correctly, on the left. "This is not what I'd call keeping up with traffic."

The town of Issaquah was behind them now. "The speed limit's sixty-five here."

"Since when?"

"Since about a mile back."

Derek twisted in his seat, craned his neck trying to see the alleged sign. "How come I missed the sign, then?"

"Beats me."

He turned front again. Sighed. Drummed his fingers on his thigh. Cleared his throat. "So. You get many speeding tickets?"

B.J. slanted him a look, and on seeing his expression, burst into laughter. "A few."

"I'm not surprised." Another deep breath. "Accidents?"

"One or two." B.J. hit the horn with the heel of her hand. "Get glasses, buster! Did you see that guy swerve into our lane?" she demanded hotly, then yelled, "Let your mother drive," as she glared into the rearview mirror.

Derek locked his knees, bracing himself in case of God-knew-what. "Nice car," he croaked.

"I like it." She passed a bus, waved at the driver.

"Get good mileage, do you?"

"Fair."

Derek fidgeted, cleared his throat again and finally couldn't stand it anymore. With a muffled oath, he jerked around to face her. "Look, it's nothing personal, but could I drive?"

"What?" B.J.'s brows shot up to her hairline.

"I said, could I—"

"I heard you the first time." A car pulled out in front of them and she abruptly switched lanes, muttering something short and unintelligible. Derek's stomach lurched. She glanced at him sideways. "You're white as a ghost. Don't tell me you're one of those men who get nervous when a woman drives?"

"Carsick, not nervous." Derek would have given a lot not to have to admit that particular failing of his. He had taken his share of ribbing about it, but the fact remained he was queasy about driving at freeway speeds at the best of times, and on winding, mountainous stretches such as these he invariably got nauseous. Especially with someone else at the wheel. "It has nothing to do with the driver's gender."

"Well, for Pete's sake." B.J. smartly pulled onto the shoulder and the car rocked to a stop. "Why didn't you say something sooner, like on the way down from Spokane, for instance? I wondered why you were acting so...so odd, but then I thought—"

"That I'm prone to acting odd?" Derek suggested mildly. Now that they were stopped, his stomach calmed and his sense of humor surfaced.

B.J. glanced at him. "Well, yes. Actually."

"Thanks," he said dryly, adding, "What it really was, was that I didn't want to risk offending you again."

"Offending me? How?"

"By asking to drive. I know that my ex-wife, for instance—"

"Don't do that," B.J. interrupted. "You're always doing that."

"What?" Derek asked, taken aback by her vehemence. He had been trying not to step on her precious feminist autonomy, for heaven's sake. "What am I always doing?"

"Making comparisons. Assumptions." One arm draped over the steering wheel, the other along the back of the seat, B.J. twisted toward him. In view of the earnestness with which she looked at him, Derek did his utmost not to be distracted by the enticing curves her position displayed, but it was damn difficult. She was casually dressed, as he was, wearing a cotton turtleneck which clung most lovingly to her slender torso and generous breasts.

"Look," she said, "I'm me, okay...?"

Boy, was she.

"...and whatever I do or say," she went on, "has nothing to do with what other women do or say. I have my own set of rules, my own guidelines by which I operate and for which I am prepared to take responsibility. Not some other woman's, all right?"

"F-fine." Derek kept his eyes on hers with herculean effort. "I apologize."

"Don't be silly," she said, magnanimous now that she had made her point. To Derek's regret-tinged relief, she faced front again and opened her door. "In the future just remember that with me you don't have to pussyfoot around." She shot him a grin and hopped out of the car. "Slide over, Mr. Coleman. You're the driver."

As soon as they were on the way again, she said, "So do you still want to stop on Snoqualmie Summit and take a few runs?"

They had discovered the previous night that they were both avid skiers. And mellow after a couple of glasses of wine, they had on the spur of the moment decided to stop and ski for a couple of hours on the way home. B.J. always carried her stuff around with her in the car during the winter. Her position was that one never knew when opportunity knocked and it would be a darn shame not to be ready for it when it did.

Derek had brought along his ski clothes because his position was that one never knew when something might go wrong. Like a car wreck, or a breakdown which might require him to hike for help in subzero temperatures. He used to be a Boy Scout; he believed in being prepared.

"You bet," he replied in answer to B.J.'s questions. He would rent boots and skis. "Unless the snow's bad, of course."

"It won't be," B.J. said. "It's been too cold for the snow to have turned into Northwest cement yet." She was referring to the heavy, wet slush which all too often passed for snow on Pacific Northwest ski hills. "I really got spoiled in Colorado, though, let me tell you. Powder!" A look of rhapsody transformed her face. "To die for!"

Derek chuckled. "Well, even at the best of times you're going to be hard-put to find powder anywhere around Snoqualmie Pass."

"Hmm. Except maybe at Alpental."

"Maybe. Up high, in the back bowls."

"Let's go there, then, shall we?"

Derek flashed her a grin. "Sure. Why not?" He was a pretty good skier; in fact, pretty *damn* good, if he might be permitted to say so himself. Maybe it was petty of him to look forward to putting the lady down a few notches. Not humiliate her, mind you, just put her in her place a tad. B. J. Rawlings seemed to be so damn good at everything else she did. And he was, after all, only human.

Chapter Three

"Lord, but I love to be up here on a day like this." With a sigh of bliss, B.J. turned her liberally sunblock-protected face toward the sun and greedily soaked up its warming rays. She and Derek were on the chair lift going up.

"You and everyone else in the world, by the looks of this place." Scowling, Derek checked his watch. "Do you realize we stood in that lift line for half an hour? At this rate we'll be lucky to get in three runs during the short time we allowed for this diversion."

"Hmm." B.J. was too happy to be bothered by Derek Coleman's harping. She loved the mountains, the trees, the snow. She loved to ski. Time was, years ago, when she and her father had dreamed of her making the Olympic team.

"Unless you want to get a room over at the Summit Inn, and stay the night," Derek added with a hopeful upswing of his voice at the end of the sentence.

The idea was tempting. B.J. grimaced with genuine regret. Her mother had been feeling pretty well when they'd talked on the phone that morning, but B.J. didn't like to leave her alone yet another night, regardless. "I'm afraid I can't," she said.

Derek's brows rose above the mirrored sunglasses he wore. "Heavy date?"

He could have immediately bitten off his tongue. What did he think he was doing, asking her a personal question like that? And why the *hell* was he holding his breath waiting for her to answer?

Forcefully he expelled the air from his lungs. "Sorry. Erase that, would you?"

"Oh, sure." B.J laughed. "That's like the judge telling the jury to forget they heard a damaging piece of evidence after some attorney did his best to make it known."

Impulsively she pushed Derek's glasses up on his forehead with a mittened hand so that she could look him in the eye. "You're pussyfooting again, Mr. Coleman," she told him, and gently let the glasses drop back down.

Derek was so completely baffled and disarmed by this woman who seemed totally lacking in the kind of guile he'd come to expect from members of her sex, that he tipped back his head and laughed aloud.

Grinning from ear to ear, totally pleased with herself for the simple reason that she had made this much-too-somber man laugh, B.J. watched him.

He sure was handsome when he loosened up. She had noticed it earlier, that morning, when he'd come down for breakfast. He hadn't slicked back his hair the way he usually did. And without whatever gel he slathered it with on a working day, it was all the colors of an otter's pelt—a whole variety of browns. It was wavy, thick and unruly, flopping this way and that. There'd been a time or two during breakfast when she'd had to all but sit on her hands so as not to reach out and smooth back the strands which curled down onto his brow.

He had wonderfully white teeth, too, she noted, watching him laugh. And she'd noticed the crisp chiseled outline of his lips right away that first night they'd met. Relaxed, that mouth of his was decidedly sensuous. By simply closing her eyes she could still conjure up the feeling of it grazing her temple as he whispered innocuous things to her as they danced.

Unbeknownst to B.J. her grin had faded so that, when Derek suddenly turned his head toward her, he caught her staring at him with an expression that instantly stilled his laughter. And had his pulse leaping.

"B.J.?" He leaned toward her as if pushed by an invisible hand.

"You should laugh more often," B.J. told him, neither moving toward him nor away. "Why don't you, Derek?"

This was the first time they'd used each other's first name, but neither noticed.

"Long story," Derek said, his mouth only inches from hers now. "And boring."

"I doubt it." His proximity was doing strange things to B.J.'s breathing, and afraid he would notice she glanced away. With relief she saw the chair lift's dismount station just ahead. With escape from Derek's nearness imminent, her emotional equilibrium returned. "I'd love to hear it sometime. For now, however—"

She wiggled forward in her seat, jumped off the lift and finished her sentence in a laughing over-the-shoulder yell as she skied down the ramp.

"—I'll see you belo-o-o-w-w..."

It wasn't until Derek was schussing downhill after her at breakneck speed that he realized not only had B.J. not answered his question, the way she skied it didn't look as if he'd be taking her down a notch anytime soon.

The lodge loosely resembled a rambling Swiss or Austrian chalet. After several hours of exercise in the frigid mountain air, it was a popular warming up and refueling stop for the skiers. B.J. and Derek were no exception.

"You're good," Derek told B.J. as they sat warming their hands around mugs of chicken soup. On the table in front of them, gigantic hamburgers waited to be consumed. "Been skiing long?" he added, tongue in cheek.

"A while." B.J. stared down into the golden broth in her mug. She always tended to be melancholy after a good skiing session because what-ifs and if-onlys invariably began to whisper in her ear.

"What happened?" Derek asked, sensing her mood, and somehow perhaps foolishly, needing to ease it. "Care to talk about it?"

B.J.'s smile was hardly more than a stretching of the lips. "There's nothing much to talk about, really," she said. She shrugged, a resigned, rather sad lifting of one shoulder. "My father was John Darren Rawlings—you might have heard of him. He was an Olympic bronze medalist in the downhill some thirty years ago. Anyway, he hoped one day I'd follow in his footsteps, except maybe get one step further. He wanted me to go for the gold."

"What happened?"

B.J.'s voice roughened. "I fell."

"Oh." Surreptitiously Derek studied her half-averted face. As always when he consciously looked at her—something he tried to avoid as much as possible for the sake of his sanity and their working relationship—he was struck by her beauty, by the purity of her features. She seemed without artifice.

She spoke and acted with a degree of forthrightness that impressed Derek, and when not up in arms about something he had said, she was prone to displaying a streak of good-natured mischievousness that was very reminiscent of Baby, his lovable Great Dane. He was sure now, too, that on the night of Morrison's party it had been this playful streak rather than malice that had prompted her to play Joanie, the stereotypical sex kitten to his Leo, the lusty lecher.

One thing he had learned over the past few days—B. J. Rawlings was no stereotype of any kind. She was her own woman, and apparently as multifaceted as a diamond.

Diamond or rhinestone? A legitimate question or merely another manifestation of rampant cynicism on his part? Was the purity, the goodness, the sparkle and shine of her real or cleverly faked?

One thing was sure, her regret—it could almost be described as sorrow—at having lost the opportunity to fulfill her father's dream was genuine.

It stirred him, made him awkwardly touch her arm. "I'm sorry."

"Don't be." She smiled a smile so bittersweet it twisted his heart. "It was always his dream more than mine. For me the pain of having disappointed him again was—"

"Again? You disappointed him a lot?"

"Not on purpose, of course, but Pop had very definite expectations and so—yeah." She shrugged, frowning a little. "It wasn't always easy being an only child. You know...?"

"Well, actually I don't know, but I can remember sometimes wishing I *were* an only child. I grew up with three brothers."

"Ah," she said softly. "All boys. Your father must've been so proud...."

She looked and sounded so wistful, saying that, that Derek was at a loss as to how to reply. Too, something told him it might be best to let it ride, and so he gave her arm another awkward pat after which, not sure what to do with his hand, he rubbed it along the side of his pants a couple of times and picked up his hamburger.

"I'm starved," he announced. "How about you?"

"Ravenous." Glad of the chance to shake off her somber mood and grateful to Derek for changing the subject, B.J. lifted her own burger to her mouth and took a healthy bite. "Deewishes," she mumbled.

They ate, breaking their quite companionable silence only with an occasional comment about the food, the snow and the fact that they had better be making tracks, since it was going on three o'clock and they had a four-hour drive yet ahead of them.

Derek figured to himself that not getting back to Spokane till seven must mean B.J. didn't have a dinner date, then impatiently brushed the speculation, as well as the conclusion, aside. People ate dinner at all hours of the evening, after all, and more importantly the entire issue was hardly his business.

Still, moments later he caught himself wondering what type of man a woman such as B. J. Rawlings dated. Someone rich and powerful, no doubt. Someone who would take her to the theater or the opera in a limousine. Who maybe slipped some expensive trinket around her neck or wrist now and then.

Derek's gaze flicked to B.J.'s fingers pushing the last bite of hamburger into her mouth. They were bare of rings except for a modest diamond on her right hand. A memento from a severed relationship?

Of course, the fact that she wore virtually no jewelry didn't mean anything. Just like Margo, B.J. had excellent taste and a sense of decorum. Flashy jewelry would be saved for evenings, for nights on the town with the man who had bestowed the loot. Insidiously, in the course of Derek's brooding, the name Floyd Morrison crept into his mind. Was there really nothing going on there? he wondered yet again. B.J. sure had been outraged.

Real outrage, or a case of protesting too much?

"If you don't mind, I'll just make a quick trip to the rest room," B.J., ignorant of Derek's black thoughts, interrupted, "and then I'm ready to leave, if you are."

"Fine."

If B.J. was taken aback by his curt tone, she didn't show it. With a quick smile at him, she rose and walked toward the door.

Derek noticed with a niggling sense of annoyance that quite a few pairs of masculine eyes followed her exit. Of course, his did, too, and to say that it was no chore would be the understatement of the century. Bertha Joanne Rawlings was one hell of a fine figure of a woman. At once slender and voluptuous, she did things to a pair of stretch ski pants that had his blood coursing eagerly and hotly through his veins.

Damn.

Almost violently Derek pushed back his chair and stood. Stalking toward the cafeteria counter to buy a cup of coffee for the road, he sternly told himself he had to stop carrying on like a pimply-faced high-school sophomore with the hots.

He was a thirty-seven-year-old man, for Pete's sake. More, in a manner of speaking he was the woman's boss or, at the very least, a professional associate. As such, as he needed to work with her, he would have to consult with her and occasionally travel with her—the same as he did with Jack Carruthers, Ross MacGuire and the others on their sales team.

He had never had trouble working alongside women before—he had always prided himself on his ability to keep his private opinions and feelings separate, to not let them intrude into working relationships. So what the hell, Derek demanded of himself—what the *hell* was his problem with the Rawlings woman?

"B.J.! Sweetheart! I thought I recognized that cute tush of yours."

At the shout, Derek turned, just in time to see "the Rawlings woman" coming back into the room and being swept into a bear hug by a tall, tanned athletic type, who then proceeded to thoroughly kiss her.

Without being aware of it, Derek crushed the disposable cup he had picked up.

"Damn but you're a sight for sore eyes," the guy was saying when he came up for air, talking loudly enough for the whole place to hear. "Where you been hidin' yourself, gorgeous? Last time I saw you was where? Aspen? Three, four years ago?" He leaned back to create enough space between them for B.J. to catch his salacious grin. "You were wearing pink long johns, babe, and sneaking along the hall in the middle of the night!" He included his table mates in the grin. "You shoulda seen her, guys..."

"I was not sneaking," B.J. protested, laughing, "you were, you big ape." She playfully and ineffectually punched the giant's bulging biceps. "*Out* of Katherine Brewster's room, I might add, in your *shorts* and at six o'clock in the morning! I, on the other hand, was merely on my way to the shower...."

"Ri-i-i-ght," the big man hammed, this time tossing his pals an over-the-shoulder wink. "We've used that line ourselves a time or two, eh, guys?"

There were shouts of agreement and laughter, which B.J. helplessly shared.

"Unless your plans for tonight have changed, Ms. Rawlings," Derek said stiffly, materializing next to her, "I think we should be leaving."

Ms. Rawlings? the giant mouthed in an outrageous pantomime, making Derek feel old and stodgy.

"Let go of me, you idiot," B.J. told her muscle-bound captor with indulgent good humor, adding with a rueful smile toward Derek, "and meet my boss, Derek Coleman. Mr. Coleman," she introduced, "Leonard Jones, ski bum."

"Ski bum?" Leonard was all twinkling outrage. "I'm a distinguished member of the M-3 demonstration ski team, I'll have you know. They pay me and everything."

"Wow!" B.J. looked suitably impressed.

"So now will you marry me?" Len said, catching her hand in his and outrageously dropping a string of little kisses along her knuckles.

"Nope."

"Cruel." Unceremoniously he dropped her hand to turn mournful eyes toward Derek. "Beautiful chicks can be so unfeeling, you know?"

Though Derek knew the man to be joking, it took some effort not to reply with a heartfelt, Boy, do I!

"Len and I go way back," B.J. said, climbing into the passenger seat of her Cherokee Jeep, because, of course, Derek would drive.

"Really." Derek busied himself with his seat belt, then shifted into reverse and backed up.

"We were on the national ski team together, before I dropped out, and we've run into each other here and there a few times since."

Where had this compulsion to explain Leonard to Derek Coleman come from? B.J. asked herself a bit indignantly. Hadn't he made it obvious he didn't care for Len? And wasn't he even now acting as if he was bored to tears? Listen to him... "I see," he said, oh so remotely, as if making a right turn and pulling out onto the access road was taking all his concentration.

And yet, something made her go right on explaining.... "He's quite a ham. Full of the devil and chasing after everything in skirts, just on principle. Every time he sees me, he proposes."

"And you always turn him down."

"Of course." She chuckled, if only to show the dark-faced man next to her that she wasn't going to let his inexplicably soured disposition infect her. "Aside from the fact that he doesn't mean it and I don't love him, I swear the only thing Leonard has ever owned in his life are his skis."

"So would you marry him if he did mean it and you did love him?"

A spark of interest! B.J. latched onto it. "Everything else being equal?" She considered a moment. "No."

"At least you're honest about your priorities." The glance Derek sent her was sardonic. "I guess that's something."

B.J. bristled. "What's that supposed to mean?"

His eyes back on the road, Derek shrugged. "Most women would have tried to wrap their response in cotton candy or prevaricated in some way or other."

"I see," B.J. said coolly, wrapping both arms tightly around herself as if to physically keep her resentment confined. She'd almost forgotten what a horse's rear this man could be. Fuming, she stared out the window on her side without seeing a thing. She should have known he would find a way to remind her of it, though. Why was it that he always seemed to expect the worst of her?

Some woman—his ex-wife?—must really have done a number on him.

Mulling that over, gradually warming to the thought, B.J.'s indignation subsided somewhat. *We're all products of our past experiences,* she conceded with grudging fairness. Didn't she carry her own load of insecurities and hang-ups around? Relaxing her rigid posture, she glanced toward her bewildering companion.

He was staring straight ahead, but he was frowning and the corner of his tightly compressed lips which was visible to B.J. formed a forbidding sort of comma. Struck by the realization that he always looked unhappy in repose, a surge of empathy made her want to reach out and with tender fingers coax the comma upward.

She didn't, of course. The nature of their relationship forbade that kind of familiar touching, but beyond that, and much more to the point, B.J. knew that eliciting a temporary smile was not the same as making him happy. Ultimately only he, himself, could do that.

B.J. sighed. Now if only she could apply all that lofty insight to herself...

"You know," she said, deciding to give the bid for mutual understanding another try, "my reasons for not being willing to marry someone like Len, even if I loved him, have to do with ambitions and goals."

"I know."

He answered so flippantly, so quickly and cynically, B.J.'s newfound sympathy all but flew out the window.

She struggled for patience. "I'm talking about his, the man's, goals and ambitions, Mr. Coleman—not mine."

In response, he only slanted her an arch look.

She refused to be ruffled. "I had a father who was hardworking and ambitious," she told him. "Skiing was great, but he felt that in the real world people made sure they could hold down real jobs, too. Jobs that went beyond the sport. Pop worked days and went to school nights to get an engineering degree. He never quite made it, but that's beside the point. What *is* the point is that he drilled into me the fact that nobody *owes* anybody anything. The only person you owe is yourself!

"You owe yourself fulfillment of your potential, which Pop, as pertained to me, translated into study, study, study. Be your own person, was another of his slogans— be 'like' nobody. Be dependent on nobody."

"Noble aspirations, I'm sure."

Again B.J.'s first reaction to Derek's dry, cynical observation was to lash out at him. How dare he cast aspersions on her father? The man had dedicated his too-short life to making her the best of everything she could be. He had expected her to be everything he was and more, and she, occasional disappointments notwithstanding, had always done her *damnedest* to fulfill his expectations.

"Since ultimately we can't change the fact that you're a girl," he had told her one day when she was about twelve, "you're going to have to work twice as hard to prove you're four times as smart as anybody else. And you are. Know it. Act on it. Never forget it."

B.J. had tried not to. Throughout grade and high schools, learning had been a breeze; it had been making friends with the other kids at which she had failed. Mandy Gordon had been her only friend, more often than not. They were still close.

In college B.J. had had to work a little harder at getting the kinds of grades her father expected, but by living on campus at least her roommates and the others on her floor had had the chance to really get to know her. Her social life had picked up some, though by and large she had always remained someone on the outside looking in.

The necessity of always having to prove herself, to show the world that a keen mind functioned beneath her too-cute-for-words exterior, might have left someone with less loving and supportive parents embittered. In B.J.'s case, their help and good example had taught her never to judge anyone on appearances, no matter how bizarre or different they might be.

But her father had been adamant in saying that second best must merely be a stepping stone to best. "If at first you don't succeed," he had liked to quote his version of that old cliché, "then you didn't work hard enough and you try again." With a wink he'd add, "And until you do succeed, act as if you already have and people will believe you."

B.J. would laugh, but she knew his words weren't meant to be funny. She had tried to follow them to the letter.

"My point was," she said to Derek, taking another deep breath for patience, "that someone like Leonard would have to demonstrate his ability to depend on no one and to live up to his potential before I'd be willing to marry him."

"What about a man's *earning* potential?" Derek persisted. "How important is that to an overachiever like you?"

One, two, three...B.J. silently prayed for forbearance. Coleman seemed determined to perceive her as some kind of hard-nosed money grubber, when dollars and cents were not what she was about at all.

"In the sense that it's an extension of everything else," she finally said, "I suppose it's *very* important. Be it ditch digging or brain surgery, by being the best at what you do it stands to reason you'd be accordingly well compensated. In other words, Mr. Coleman, it's not the dollar amount earned I consider important, but the striving to do the best you can. In my view, the Leonard Joneses of the world, rich *or* poor, don't strive toward anything but a good time. And *that's* the reason I could never marry him—or anyone else like him."

B.J. fell silent, inwardly vowing that if Derek Coleman made just one more disparaging crack, forbearance be damned—she'd deck him.

"If you genuinely believe all that rhetoric you've been spouting, Ms. Rawlings," Derek said after a while, "then you really *are* different."

"There you go generalizing and making comparisons again," B.J. exclaimed, exasperated. "I really resent that. I mean, different from what? Than who? Your ex-wife?"

She debated if she dared go on, but then decided Derek had certainly had no qualms about getting personal with her. She shifted in her seat so that she half faced him. "Maybe if you told me about her..."

Derek's brow lowered. He said nothing. With an inward sigh, B.J. decided he wasn't going to answer. She was about to withdraw the question, when he said, "She's a lot like you, you know."

His tone was not complimentary, and the glance he slanted her when she didn't reply right away was mocking. "What, no pithy comeback?"

"Actually, I was thinking that so far your ex-wife sounds perfectly wonderful."

For a moment B.J.'s blasé tone and innocent expression took Derek aback, and then he broke up. "Bertha Joanne Rawlings," he said, laughing aloud, "I just might grow to like you."

Chapter Four

B.J. was shrugging out of her heavy winter coat as she wound her way toward the table where Amanda Gordon Jenks sat perusing the menu.

"Sorry I'm late." She tossed the coat onto an empty chair and leaned down to touch cheeks with the other woman before collapsing into a chair of her own. "Phew. What a mess out there."

"Tell me about it. If not for the fact that I haven't seen you since you moved back to town, I might've canceled."

"We saw each other Christmas—"

"For about half an hour."

"—and we've talked on the phone."

"Hardly the same as a good face-to-face." Mandy took in B.J.'s tailored suit and French-braided hair. "I must say, B. J. Rawlings, you look every inch the successful professional woman."

"And you, Mandy Gordon—" B.J. relaxed against the backrest and studied her longtime friend "—look fantastic. Is it the haircut?"

Mandy touched the short bob. "Maybe." She grinned. "On the other hand, it could be the fact that I'm pregnant."

"Again?" As Mandy's brows arched, B.J. backpedaled. "I didn't mean that the way it sounded. I guess it, well, you already have the two, and Jessica is already, what? Five? That's a big gap—"

"Six."

"Jessie's six?" B.J. pulled a face. "You mean I forgot my godchild's birthday? Again?"

"Again. But not by much, this time. Only about ten days, in fact."

"March third, of course. Darn. What with my new job... And I was out of town till Saturday night."

"Really?"

"On business, Amanda."

"Of course. What else?" Mandy's tone was dry. "But till Saturday night?"

"We stopped to ski for a few hours."

"We?"

"My boss and I."

"Another career woman like yourself?"

"No."

With an intrigued "Ah," Mandy leaned expectantly across the table. "So tell me, already."

"Down, girl. There's nothing to tell."

"There never is," Mandy grumbled, subsiding back in her chair.

B.J. shot her a look. "We're discussing your life, not mine." She glanced at her watch and picked up the menu. "I have an appointment in an hour—we'd better order."

They did, and laid the menus aside.

"So you're pregnant again," B.J. marveled, returning to their earlier conversation. "Is Ron as happy about it as you obviously are?"

Mandy shrugged. "He left the decision up to me, since—as he put it—I'll be the one stuck in the house for another six years."

"And are you?"

"Am I what?"

"Stuck?"

"No." Looking at B.J., Mandy's face softened. "You know all I ever wanted was to be a mom and a housewife. I'm not smart like you, never was."

"Sometimes I think you're a heck of a lot smarter," B.J. said with a touch of melancholy. "You've got your life all figured out, a home, a family of your own. A guy who's crazy about you, while I—" She broke off, pulling a face. "In another month I'll be thirty. I guess I've been hearing the proverbial ticking of the clock a bit lately."

"Exactly why I decided that if I was gonna have another kid, now's the time. Not that there's any reason a woman can't be just as happy without kids," Mandy hastened to add after a quick look at B.J.'s glum expression. "It's just that I don't seem to be one of those, and what with Jessie starting school soon and—shoot, what would I do with myself all day? I'd go nuts rattling around the house waiting..."

She stopped, looking chagrined, and touched B.J.'s arm. "I blew it, didn't I? Ron's right, I've got foot-in-mouth disease...."

"Don't be ridiculous," B.J. said crossly, though it was herself she was cross with for having invited this bout of guilt and sympathy. "I'm hardly an object of pity, and we've always been up-front with each other. So sometimes I'm jealous of you, of what you have—so what? It passes."

She picked up her glass of water, noticed that her hand shook and set it back down.

"Sometimes I'm jealous of you, too," Mandy said. "All the people you meet, places you go, fancy restaurants you get to eat in. It's so glamorous."

B.J. snorted. "Glamorous. Oh, brother. Hard work is what it is."

They were silent a moment, then Mandy said, "So do you ever wish..." With a rueful little laugh, she let the question trail away unfinished, dismissing it with a quiet, "I s'pose not."

Their salads and diet sodas arrived. "Anything else I can get you ladies right now?" asked the waiter, then withdrew at their negative responses.

"Do I ever wish what?" B.J. asked, spooning dressing over her greens as Amanda, looking chagrined again, did the same.

"Nothing, I just wondered..." And then, as if fed up with herself and her hedging, Mandy abruptly set down her spoon. "Whatever became of Mark Quentin? Do you know?"

"Oh." B.J. took a deep breath, setting the salad dressing aside. "You were wondering if I ever wish I'd gone ahead and married him, is that it?"

Mandy half shrugged. "You were inseparable that summer. It stands to reason you'd think about him now and then."

"We were young. It's been years."

"Twenty-two's not so young. I already had a year-old kid by then."

"You're different. You yourself said earlier you never wanted a degree, a career. I, on the other hand..."

B.J. let the sentence fade, remembering that summer seven years ago. Her father had died in March, just a couple of months before her graduation from Washington State where she had studied engineering in deference to her father's wishes. Left to do her own choosing, she would have majored in liberal arts, maybe English....

But of course Pop had been right, neither of those majors would have led to anywhere near the kind of lucrative jobs she had been fortunate enough to have been offered.

That summer, too, the job she had taken at a local engineering firm had been previously lined up for her by her father. She had done some manual and computer drafting there, garnering hands-on experience before going on to graduate school in Seattle.

Mark Quentin had been one of the engineers there. Tall and lanky, very studious and intent in a dark, brooding way, he hadn't looked anything like her father, but he had seemed precisely what she needed just then. He had the most beautiful eyes, the color of molasses, large and liquid like those of a deer. His hair was long and wavy and always rumpled.

To her he had looked like a poet, and that had appealed to her. But his thinking had been all engineer—logical, methodical, linear; the kind of thinking B.J. was used to from her father. After her recent loss, she had found that appealing, too.

Mark hadn't come on to her, either, the way most of the other young engineers there felt compelled to do. He had treated her as he treated everybody else, a little rudely. He got away with it because he was brilliant, and B.J. had been thrilled to death when he singled her out during discussions, or gave her some work to do. Drudge work, tedious calculations, stuff—so she found out later—he considered not worthy of his time, but always took the credit for having done.

B.J. had felt flattered by the attention he paid her at work, and by the time he asked her out she had been head over heels and ripe for the plucking. She had lost her virginity on their first date, if it could be called a date. He had asked her to have dinner with him at his place, which meant he'd tossed a frozen pizza into the oven and B.J. into bed.

There'd been no hosannas for her. In truth there had been none of the wondrous feelings B.J.'s limited romantic reading had led her to expect. Not the first time, nor at any subsequent time. Sex, she found out, was quick and to the point, and in her opinion highly overrated as a recreational activity.

Marriage was mentioned a few weeks before summer's end. Mark was going on to get his Ph.D. He took it for granted that B.J. would work and earn money while he went on to earn his doctorate. He'd pressed for a commitment from B.J. which, when it came right down to it, she'd been unable to make.

Her mother said this proved that B.J. didn't really love Mark, and on the surface B.J. had concurred. But during those times when she was being honest with herself, she knew it hadn't been as simple as that. Fear, more than lack of love, had kept her from making that commitment. Fear of failure, fear of loss, fear of the kind of intimacy that allows another person to know every last thing about you.

Even now, faced with the prospect of never having the things for which she professed to envy Mandy Jenks, B.J. knew that given another chance she would make the same choices.

Someone told her once that surely she had it all—beauty, brains and a job she loved. B.J. had smiled and nodded—and she had marveled at how well outward appearances were able to deceive other people.

Did she wish she had married Mark? No. Would she tell Mandy, who knew her far better than anyone, all of her reasons why? Again, no.

"Neither Mark nor I was done with school," she said evasively.

"You had your bachelor's."

"True. But I'd promised Pop I'd go for a master's, at least. Mark wanted me to shelve my own postgraduate plans and get a job. I had to make choices...."

"And Mark lost."

"I wonder." B.J. could see Mandy was taken aback by what must seem to her like cold-bloodedness on B.J.'s part. Well, B.J. told herself grimly, at least Mandy was in good company. Derek Coleman had reached a similar conclusion and he didn't know her half as well as Mandy did. Maybe it was true.

"I'm sure he's better off without me." She resolutely switched to a lighter tone. "I mean, think of it, Amanda—down the road a bit, the man wanted children. Can you see it? Me, the absolutely most inept and nonmaternal woman in the world, have children?"

"Mike and Jessie adore you."

"And I adore them. But, then, how much can a person mess up in a few short hours?"

Their eyes met and they both cracked up. "Plenty," they said in unison, as several calamities involving Mandy's kids and B.J.'s baby-sitting abilities came to mind.

"Remember the time I made popcorn with them?"

"How could I forget? To this day my favorite pot has black kernels welded to its bottom and I can't pass a fire extinguisher without shuddering. What a mess!"

"Yuck." B.J., too, gave a reminiscent shudder. "Mark can thank his lucky stars I didn't inflict myself on him. Not only am I awkward with kids, I'm a dud in the kitchen—pretty much an all-around slob—and the only thing I enjoy doing out in the yard is napping in the shade of a tree."

Mandy shook her head. "There's a lot more to marriage than housework, kids and gardening, girl. You can hire people for that. It's the sharing of your troubles—"

"I've got you and Mom for that."

"There's intimacy."

"Yes, well..." B.J. felt her cheeks grow hot and busied herself with a dinner roll.

"I mean as in talking and being close emotionally, not just sex." Mandy leaned across the table. "Though speaking of which—"

"Let's not, all right?" Good grief, B.J. thought, that's all she needed—a discussion of her sex life, or lack of it, over tossed green salads. She pushed her plate away, glanced at her watch again. "Goodness, I'm almost out of time."

"Look," she said, changing the subject, "I'd like to do something with the kids for Jessie's birthday, something even I can handle. Like maybe take them to a movie. What's a good day?"

"Saturdays or Sundays are good."

"Great." B.J. thought it best to ignore her friend's disgruntled expression. As far as Mandy was concerned, every woman twenty-one or over ought to be married, and those who weren't just *had* to be either promiscuous or sexually frustrated.

B.J. was neither. She'd been intimate with only two men in her life, and there hadn't been anyone for several years now. It didn't matter—both of her lovers, one of them Mark, had let her know that her talents quite obviously lay elsewhere. Since B.J. knew that this "elsewhere" wasn't the kitchen or nursery any more than the bedroom, she'd made up her mind to concentrate her energies on where her talents did lie: the business world.

Not everyone could be dynamite in bed or homemaker extraordinaire, B.J. told herself, and she, for one, could live quite happily without knocking herself out to be either.

She suppressed a sigh, thinking she really could do without all this soul-searching, too. It seemed that ever since she'd moved back to Spokane, things from the past had been tripping her up. Issues she hadn't stewed about in years came creeping out of the dark corners and crevices of her mind to which they'd been relegated, and demanded attention and examination.

So, was it her impending thirtieth birthday, or was coming up against Derek Coleman making her emotional equilibrium go topsy-turvy?

As quickly as the question had reared its ugly head, B.J. tamped it back down and dredged up a smile for her friend. "Why don't we hope today's blizzard is this winter's swan song and plan for the weekend after next? I'll let you know whether Saturday or Sunday would be better."

"Sounds good." Mandy's eyes went beyond B.J. "Don't look now, but there's a man staring holes into the back of your head."

Much to Mandy's obvious disgust, B.J. promptly craned her neck and saw Derek Coleman standing near the cash register. Wearing a camel hair overcoat, his cheeks ruddy and his hair mussed from the wind, he was a sight that could easily gladden a maiden's heart.

B.J. willed her own not to beat faster and her face not to flush. She acknowledged him with a brisk nod and turned back to Mandy.

"That's not a man," she said coolly, "that's my boss. And those piercing looks of his mean it's time for me to go."

"He sure looks like a man to me," Mandy said, pulling money out of her purse to cover her share of the bill, as B.J. was doing. "And time to go or not, he's coming over here." She shot B.J. a grin. "Oh, goody, I'll get to meet him."

Just dandy, B.J. thought, flushing now, in spite of her resolve not to, and being bombarded by speculative glances from Amanda Gordon Jenks as a consequence. She plunked some bills onto the table and rose. The more she was ready to leave, the shorter Mandy's time with Derek Coleman would be.

"Allow me." Derek was holding B.J.'s coat for her to slip into.

B.J. did so somewhat grudgingly. Coleman's little bouts of chivalry always threw her. She could manage her own coat, for heaven's sake. On the other hand, she was honest enough to admit that occasionally having a door held for her and such did make her feel . . . feminine.

Her lips curved. "Thank you."

"You're welcome." His smile was every bit as brief and impersonal as B.J.'s had been.

He turned to Mandy, who had also risen, and he held out his hand. "Derek Coleman," he introduced himself.

"Amanda Jenks." They shook hands, doing some quick sizing up.

"Mandy is an old friend of mine," B.J. explained.

"Doesn't look so old to me," Derek said gallantly, and they all duly chuckled.

"Old, as in longtime," Mandy elaborated. "As in all the way back to junior high school."

"I see."

They all stood awkwardly a moment, the way people who didn't know each other on a personal level and who had run out of chitchat were prone to do.

As if on cue, B.J. and Derek both jerked back a sleeve and checked their watches.

"Goodness—"

"Well—"

They exchanged purposeful glances.

"Shall we?" Derek said.

"I think we'd better."

B.J. turned to Amanda. "It's been lovely, Mandy. I'll give you a call about—"

"Oh, I've got to get going, too. The kids..." Mandy picked her faux-fur jacket off yet another chair.

"You have children?" Derek took the coat from her and helped her into it.

"Yes. Thank you. Two." Mandy tossed B.J. an innocent smile. "B.J., here, is their godmother. She *loves* children."

"Really?" Derek glanced at B.J., who was struggling with the urge not to give her friend a swift kick in the shins.

The urge increased a hundredfold when Mandy asked, "And do you have children, Mr. Coleman?"

"Afraid not."

"But you *are* married, surely?"

B.J.'s glare told Mandy she was dead meat.

"Divorced," Derek said absently, once again consulting his watch. "Ms. Rawlings, time's getting tight."

"You're going together?" Mandy asked, falling in behind B.J. who was already hurrying toward the exit.

"Only to this particular appointment, Amanda," B.J. informed her somewhat testily across one shoulder.

"I came by cab." Mandy cast a glance back at Derek, who was bringing up the rear. "I wonder...are the two of you going past my house, by any chance? The weather, you know..."

"Are we, Ms. Rawlings?"

Unfortunately they were. "Yes, I believe so."

"Then we'll be glad to give you a lift."

B.J. had already sailed out through the door on her own, her exasperation with Mandy like wind in her sails. Her motions jerky with displeasure, she tugged on lined leather gloves and flipped up the hood of her long winter coat.

If anything, it was snowing harder than it had before lunch, and the temperatures seemed to have dropped, too. Talk about March coming in like a lion!

"Where are you parked?" she asked Derek, ignoring Mandy's Cheshire cat grin.

"Right next to you, over there." Head down against the wind, he led the way.

"Nice guy," Mandy whispered to B.J.

"Oh, shut up."

"A Beemer, wow!" Mandy slid a gloved finger along the side of Derek's silvery taupe five-hundred-series BMW. "Ron would trade both of our kids and me for one of these."

Derek chuckled, holding the rear door for her to climb in. "Just goes to show," he said. "Me, I'd trade this car for a wife and two kids of my own in a minute."

He turned in time to close B.J.'s door behind her, rounded the hood and got in behind the wheel.

"Are we nuts to be driving out to Wanger's in this blizzard or what?" he muttered, starting the engine without removing his gloves. "It'll be warm in here in a minute."

They sat a moment, waiting for the engine to warm up and the front and rear window defrosters to do their job.

B.J. was frowning, her mind on Derek's remark. "If you're worried about it, we could postpone the appointment, or we could take the Cherokee."

"And let you drive? No, thanks."

"I don't care who *drives*, Mr. Coleman—"

"Well, I do. Me." He slammed into reverse, giving B.J. a so-there glance before backing out of the stall. "As to postponing, you forget we're already three days late getting them these drawings."

"You're right."

"Besides which, old man Wanger is nervous about doing business with a woman. If you cancel he'll say 'See?'"

"You're right." B.J. sighed, remembering a recent telephone conversation she had with the man. Thank God, he was in the minority out there these days. Most of the men she dealt with in the line of business had no problems with her gender, or if they did, they had learned not to let it show. "It's good of you to come along and help me ease Mr. Wanger into the twentieth century," she said dryly.

"Ease, hell. He'll kick and scream all the way." They were pulling out into traffic, and the front wheels spun a bit and the car's back end swerved before the tires got a grip on the hard-packed snow.

"You okay back there, Mrs. Jenks?" Derek asked with a quick glance at Mandy in the rearview mirror.

"Good grief, call me Mandy. And yes, I'm fine." She settled more comfortably into the plush back seat. "I doubt I would've gotten a taxi, so I really appreciate the ride."

"No problem. Glad to do it."

The car was moving along without problem and it was warm inside now, too. B.J. removed her gloves, drew off the hood and opened her coat.

"Mandy, I know Mikey's probably in school," she said, shifting sideways as much as the seat belt allowed, so that she could more easily look back at her friend as they spoke. The fact that Derek Coleman's chiseled profile thus also happened to be in her direct line of vision was a nice bonus. It seemed to B.J. he grew more handsome each time she saw him, which, of course, was neither here nor there and just an observation. "Where'd you leave Jessica today?"

"With Ron at the station. My husband owns a service station and garage," Mandy elaborated for Derek's benefit, adding, "He's real good with European cars, and reasonable, too. You might want to think of him next time your car needs service."

"Nice to see a wife trying to further her husband's interests."

Mandy's shrug was unapologetic. "I guess it goes with the territory."

"Hardly." Derek's chuckle was without humor, and neither, B.J. noted, was he smiling. "If you'll tell me where he's located, I'll keep him in mind."

"Great. In fact, just drop me off there today and you'll see it for yourself. Ron's a great mechanic, isn't he, B.J.?"

"The best."

"See?" Mandy beamed. "And she isn't just saying that because she went to school with him, either."

"College?" Derek asked with a quick glance at B.J.

She shook her head. "High school. Ron was a defensive tackle on our football team."

"Ah. A big guy, huh?"

B.J. and Mandy exchanged smiling glances. "Real *big*," they chorused. "And quite the local hero," B.J. added.

"With the two of you cheering him on, no doubt."

"If you mean, were B.J. and I cheerleaders—I'm afraid not. I was too nerdy and B.J. wasn't allowed."

"Oh?"

"Her father thought it was frivolous. He was real strict."

"He felt academics were more important than jumping up and down on a football field, Amanda," B.J. said, defensive in the face of Derek Coleman's pensive expression. "And you know darn well I didn't want to be on that cheering squad in the first place."

"That's because the other girls were all so mean to you."

"Amanda...!"

"Well, they were. Because the guys were always making cow eyes at B.J.," Mandy explained to Derek, ignoring B.J.'s fulminating glare. "B.J. hated that, and all the girls hated her."

"Except you." He said it quietly.

"Well, like I said, I was a nerd. I was no threat to anybody—the guys didn't look at me, anyway. Except Ron." With a little laugh she added, "I still don't know why."

Watching in the rearview mirror as merriment transformed Mandy's rather ordinary face into a special one, Derek thought that Ron sounded remarkably astute.

B.J. voiced his thoughts. "Because Ron's no dummy, that's why," she said. "He knew you were the best, just like I do." She shot her friend an arch glance. "Usually."

"So what did you do for fun in your youth, Ms. Rawlings?" Presented with the opportunity to learn a few things about his beauteous and standoffish district sales manager, things that wouldn't be found in résumés and personnel files and which she wouldn't volunteer, Derek vowed to milk it for all it was worth.

Since their conversation on the way back from Seattle, he had thought often about the things she'd said. He found himself wanting to know who had shaped her thinking and attitudes and how they had come about.

Right now he figured Amanda Jenks could certainly shed some light on this very intriguing subject.

He wasn't wrong. "Nothing," Mandy said disgustedly.

That earned her a glower from B.J. "I spent a lot of time with my father," she said tightly. "We did many wonderful things together."

"Things like...?" Derek prompted, not oblivious to the fact that she was twisting her gloves into a corkscrew on her lap.

"He taught me things. Stuff around the house that needed fixing. Model airplanes... Some of the ones we built won prizes. In the summer we hiked or went mountain climbing. We did Mount Rainier one summer."

"How old were you then?"

"Sixteen." This from Mandy. "I remember, because that's the summer I went to my Aunt Gert's at Priest Lake and you couldn't come because your Dad had you training all the time for that climb."

"He'd been looking forward to it," B.J. defended. "And he did feel bad about Priest Lake. Remember, he took both of us camping and fishing on Lake Coeur D'Alene Labor Day weekend to make up for it."

"I remember." Mandy sounded glum. "I got poison ivy."

"Next you'll be blaming Pop for that, too."

One look at B.J.'s set face and Derek knew it was time to change the subject. "How close are we to your place, Mrs. Je—, uh, Mandy? I can't see more than a few feet in front of us."

"Let's see, where are we?" She peered out into the swirling snow. "Oliver and State Street. Take a right at the next corner and two blocks up you'll see the station."

It seemed they slid more than drove over to Ron's Auto Service, as the Jenks's business was named. Derek saw that the women had not exaggerated. Ron was *big*. Six foot four or five, weighing two-fifty easy, not all of it muscle any longer, nor situated quite where it once had been. But for all that he was built like a brick outhouse, his ready smile and expansive manner left no doubt that he had the mellow disposition of a cuddly teddy bear.

He enveloped his wife in a mighty hug, chucked B.J. under the chin with a grease-stained finger, leaving a mark, and shook Derek's hand with ready bonhomie.

"Great car you got there, Coleman. If you need 'er serviced, why—"

"I already gave him the pitch, hon," Mandy interrupted. "And they're late for an appointment." She tottered as a screeching towhead launched herself at Mandy's midsection. "Jessie!" She swung the child up in her arms. "Just in time to kiss your Auntie B.J. bye-bye."

"I don't wanna," the child wailed. "I want Auntie B.J. to sta-a-y-y...."

"You know what," Derek said to Ron, "if I could just use your phone, I think I'll check on that appointment of ours. It's getting so miserable out there, I wouldn't be surprised if the company we were planning to call on didn't close early.''

"Right through there in the office. Help yourself."

As Derek went to the phone, Mandy opened the car door and put the little girl on B.J.'s lap. "Tell her," she mouthed with a meaningful look.

"Um..." Though her arms closed around the small body automatically, B.J. was at a loss for a second as to what to say.

"The weekend..." Mandy prompted soundlessly.

"Oh. Yes. Jessie," B.J. murmured, nudging the warm face pressed into the crook of her neck with her chin. "I got you a birthday present—"

"Where is it?" Up came the head.

"At my house. But I'll bring it over on the weekend," B.J. quickly tagged on, when Jessica's face began to cloud again.

"What is it?"

B.J. leaned close and whispered in Jessie's ear.

Derek, sticking his head in the door on the driver's side, noted that their hair, mingling as they stuck their heads together, was almost the identical silvery blond shade.

"Ms. Rawlings," he said, just as Jessica popped back to give B.J. a gap-toothed grin and squealed, "Really? And does it tell time and everything?"

"You betcha."

"And will you bring it Saturday?"

"Right after breakfast."

"And will you stay all day?"

"I think Mom would kick me out if I did. How about we go to the movies?"

"Ya-a-y-y—" She stopped in mid-yell, eyes wide on Derek whom she had obviously just spotted.

"Hi," he said with a wink.

Suddenly shy, Jessica hid her face in B.J.'s neck again, only to peek out at him a second later. "Hi."

"So you like to go to the movies, huh?"

"Yes. And my brother does, too," she added, shyness forgotten. "He's eight. I used to be five but I had a birthday and now I'm six."

"Wow," Derek said, duly impressed. "I guess I should have brought a present for you then, huh?"

"You could bring it Saturday..."

"Jessica!" both B.J. and Mandy exclaimed. B.J. with horror at the very idea of spending yet another precious day off in Derek Coleman's company, Mandy by way of reprimand.

"Well, he could," the child insisted, as Derek laughed.

"Maybe I'll see you at the park or at the movie," he said, "if your Aunt B.J. will tell me where you'll be, but meanwhile—"

He leaned across the driver's seat, his shoulder brushing B.J.'s and his scent enveloping her, and opened the glove compartment. He took something out, but didn't straighten. Instead, he turned his head so that his face almost touched B.J.'s. "How about this book for a present?"

"Animals, neat-o," Jessie exclaimed.

"What do you say?" B.J. prompted softly, her eyes on Derek, whose gaze shifted back and forth between herself and her goddaughter. "Do you always carry around birthday presents in your car?" she asked.

"Always," he murmured, his eyes now on her mouth.

B.J.'s face burned.

"Thank you," Jessica caroled.

"Mr. Coleman," Mandy prompted.

"Thank you, Mr. Coleman," Jessie repeated.

"You're welcome, Jessica."

The child scampered off B.J.'s lap and ran to her mother. "Look, Mom..."

Derek stayed where he was. "I called Wanger, but all I got was an answering service. Seems they left for the day, due to the weather. I think we'd be smart to get going, too."

"O-of course." Did he have to be so close? And so warm? "The sooner, the better."

B.J. drew a breath of relief when he pulled back and straightened, but his cologne and his warmth lingered on. They said their goodbyes rather hurriedly and quickly got under way.

For a while they drove in silence, Derek concentrating on keeping the car on track on the now all but deserted country road, B.J. brooding about the tumultuous feelings that overcame her whenever she spent more than a few minutes of nonbusiness time with the man next to her.

She was drawn to him and she didn't want to be. It was that simple and that complicated.

It was this attraction that had her dredging up ghosts and fears and insecurities from the past, and she didn't much want that, either.

Derek Coleman made her wonder, made her doubt. Made her wish and long. She wanted that least of all.

"Holy sh—!" Derek's teeth clamped down on his lower lip and cut short the epithet. It was all he could do to keep the crazily swerving car from doing a waltz across the width of the road.

Startled out of her reverie, B.J. gripped the dash, blinking. "What happened?"

Derek didn't answer, nor had B.J. expected him to. She could see he was busy getting the car out of its spin and expelled a sigh of relief when he succeeded—just seconds before the Beemer slid sideways into a shallow ditch.

Chapter Five

"What happened?" B.J. repeated, dazed and—thanks to the slightly leftward tilt of the ditched car—with her shoulder pressed firmly against Derek Coleman's.

Derek's only reply was a quelling glare before he snapped off the engine and just naturally slumped—again, thanks to gravity—against the door on his side. After a moment of dark reflection, he pronounced, "We're stuck."

"Swell." Just what she needed, B.J. thought, more quality time with Derek Coleman and all that entailed in terms of heart palpitations on her part.

"What...I mean—" She bit her lip, trying to think of something helpful to say, but what came out was another "But *what happened?*"

"Is that all you can say?"

A sense of outrage, quite out of proportion to B.J.'s "crime" of asking a stupid question, but welcome, had Derek jerking upright and away from his door as best he could under the circumstances. The motion sharply jostled B.J.'s shoulder, which, in turn, had her immediately scrambling back to her side of the car. She hung onto the grip on the door to keep herself there.

That made Derek even madder. "I thought I saw something on the road," he snapped, "and I slammed on the brake, is what happened, all right?"

"All right." B.J. murmured the words as inoffensively as she could. She didn't need to be told this would not be a good time to point out none of this would have happened if she'd been driving her four-by-four Jeep.

"So now what?" she could not keep herself from asking. It was getting dark, and with the engine off it was rapidly getting cold inside the car.

"So now we wait." Grimly, Derek turned up the collar of his coat and stared straight ahead out the windshield. The subtle scent B.J. wore filled his nostrils as it had for as long as she'd been in the car, and as it did whenever circumstances required them to be in each other's company.

Ordinarily he could cope with it. With nothing to distract him, however, it caused his mind to conjure up such things as the softness of her cheeks and temple against his lips when they'd danced. The feel of her body in his arms. Her thigh brushing against his, her hands...

"Lord, I wish I'd gone to the bathroom back at Ron's."

The rather wistful pronouncement brought Derek back to reality *fast*. He stared at her, aghast. "What?"

B.J sighed. "Never mind. I can wait."

"We could be here all night, for heaven's sake."

She shrugged, and with a twinkling sideways glance at him said, "If we are, I'll just have to get out and do it in the ditch. You'll find my father didn't raise a shrinking violet."

"Somehow I'm not surprised."

"Meaning?"

A loaded question if ever Derek heard one. And since he had long since figured out that B.J.'s feelings for her father were strong, and he was in no mood to have his head shot off by enemy fire, he chose his words carefully.

"Meaning, I suppose, that your father was consistent. Meaning, he took you camping, hiking, skiing, fishing *and* mountain climbing—all the things a father likes to do with his son—and he taught you not to be squeamish about the call of nature." He shrugged, jostling her, since she'd let go of the grip and slid against him again. "I think that's great."

B.J. drew away to eye him with suspicion. "You do?"

"Absolutely."

A warm smile rewarded him. "You know, regardless of what Mandy thinks, my father was really a nice man."

Derek's heart contracted at her earnest tone. He wondered who she was trying to convince—him or herself? "I'm sure he was."

She shivered.

Derek lifted his arm and tucked her under it. "We may be here for a while," he explained. To himself or to her? "I think we'd better combine body heat."

That made it all right. No, B.J. assured herself while willing her pulse to stay normal, that didn't just make it all right, that made it *imperative* she cooperate.

She hesitated only briefly before snuggling closer against his solid warmth. "He wanted me to be the best," she murmured, "at everything I did."

"And were you?"

"I tried to be."

"And you're still trying, aren't you?"

"Hmm." She burrowed closer. "This is nice."

"I doubt you'll think so tomorrow, when you think back on this," Derek muttered. Something in him wished he were wrong, even as he knew he was right.

"How come you don't have a car phone?" B.J. roused herself to ask. Lord, but it felt good to be cozy. So good she could almost convince herself this wasn't her boss she was cuddling with, and that it wasn't just the need to share body heat that had brought them together. "If you had one, you could call for help now."

"My last holdout against progress," Derek said, tucking her in more tightly.

"And look what it got you."

Derek peered down into her face. Into her eyes. "Yeah," he breathed, slowly lowering his head. "Look what it got me, Ms. Rawlings. You. In my arms."

And then he kissed her.

It wasn't a peck, nor was it a tentative touching of mouth to mouth. It wasn't a polite, getting acquainted kind of kiss. It was a hard kiss, demanding and hungry.

It was a kiss that shocked B.J. right out of her boots.

For the length of one heartbeat everything in her stiffened in surprise and resistance—and then melted in surrender. A hunger that was every bit as strong as Derek's seized her. Her hand came up and gripped the back of his head. She braced her feet against the floorboard and pushed herself up higher on the seat, closer to the mouth to which her lips now desperately clung.

A groan, raw and needy, came up from somewhere. Hers? Derek's? It was swallowed by them both.

Swirls of delicious sensations made B.J.'s blood fizz in her veins like champagne. And never, *never* had her heart beat this fast before. It was a wild thing in her chest, just as she was rapidly becoming a wild thing in Derek's arms.

She felt his hand tunneling between them, seeking the buttons on her thick woolen coat. She shifted to accommodate him, and when he touched her breast—oh, how she wished she were naked.

Derek wished she were, too. He felt the hardened nub of her nipple through the fabric of her suit, cupped the straining roundness that fit so perfectly in the palm of his hand and wished they were anywhere but in his car with someone knocking on the window.

Someone knocking...?

Another groan, this one of pain, rose up from his quivering gut as he wrenched his lips from B.J.'s.

"No..." she protested faintly, nuzzling his throat in search of his mouth.

Derek, his eyes connecting through the passenger window with Ron Jenks's apologetic ones, could have wept. She was so sweet, so warm, so willing in his arms.

And she'd be so horrified, so cold, so regretful in just another second.

Ron had discreetly stepped away from the window and Derek saw him climb into the cab of his tow truck. The flashing lights on top of the truck were like psychedelic beacons that all too soon heralded the end of their passionate interlude.

"B.J." Derek squeezed his eyes closed in an agony of desire, which her nibbling lips along his jaw continued to stoke. "Sweetheart," he managed to say, "we've been rescued."

"Hmm," B.J. breathed, nibbling on an earlobe, intoxicated by the scent, the feel, the taste of this man. "Rescued..." She'd been rescued from the sensory sterility of her life—rescued from loneliness, from barrenness, from cold nights in cold beds, rescued from—

"What?" She lifted her head as Derek's words penetrated the delirium of her passion. She stared into his face and read regret in his pained expression even before she felt his hand gently pushing in order to create some space between them.

Sweet mercy, what had she done?

With a tiny cry of dismay, she jerked away from him. She scooted back into her corner as best she could, one hand hanging onto the grip for all she was worth, the other clutching the front of her coat.

"How could you?" she whispered hoarsely. "How *could* you?"

She was asking the question more of herself than of Derek, but he had no way of knowing that. All he knew was that his morbid premonition had been right on target—the barriers between them would be higher than ever after this. He could see the wheels already spinning in her head, could almost hear her self-recriminations.

Her head was turned to the side, in profile to him. Her eyes were closed, her lower lip quivered. "I'm so ashamed."

Now *that* Derek couldn't allow. "You were wonderful," he told her huskily. He gently touched her cheek. "More wonderful than I could possibly have imagined."

She flinched as if burned and he drew his hand away. "Look," he said quietly, "Ron is waiting to pull us out of here. We'll talk later, all right?"

But they hadn't talked. Not on the ride into town, with the three of them squeezed into the cab of Ron's truck and Derek's car in tow, and not when they parted company—at B.J.'s insistence—in the restaurant parking lot. The snow had lessened to a light flurry and the streets of the city were navigable. B.J. just wanted to be alone.

It was getting dark when she pulled into the narrow driveway next to the house. Smoke rose from the chimney, the lights shone warmly out onto the snow-covered yard and as she stepped from the car the smell of good home cooking wafted toward her from the house. And yet she didn't want to go in.

She didn't want to see her mother, or maybe it was that she didn't want to be seen. Surely she must look well kissed. Surely the momentous emotions that had rocked her only an hour ago must still be visible to her mother's discerning eye. Surely the remorse and devastation she was feeling right now would be evident.

She considered getting back in the car and leaving. But where would she go?

She would have liked to find someone to talk to. But who?

The porch door creaked. She still hadn't oiled it. "B.J.?" her mother's voice called. "B.J.! I thought I heard your car pull into the drive. Why are you standing out there in the cold, sweetheart?"

Sweetheart, Derek Coleman had called her that, too. His voice had been little more than a whisper, rough and urgent. B.J.'s heart fluttered and painfully skipped a beat before she told herself, Stop it. Men say those things to women they've just made out with. Honey, babe, sugar, sweetheart... rote endearments, meaningless tags.

"B.J.?" A note of alarm now raised her mother's voice an octave.

"Coming, Mother."

"What are you doing, child?" Bertie fussed, taking B.J.'s coat and hanging it on the three-legged coat tree in the hall. "You could catch your death."

"Actually it's not that cold out there anymore, Mom." B.J. started up the stairs to her room. "I think the wind's shifted and we'll go into a thaw."

"That'd suit me. Dinner's almost ready," Bertie called after B.J.'s retreating figure.

"I'm going to take a bath, all right? Give me half an hour."

Half an hour, Derek told himself, that's all he needed with her. Surely in that time he could make her see what had become clear to him in the course of one shattering kiss: something important was happening between them, and it deserved a chance.

Half an hour, hell—make that fifteen minutes, he was a salesman, wasn't he? Fifteen minutes, tops, and he'd have her sold.

If only she would listen.

He padded barefoot into the bedroom, briskly toweling his hair.

"Get off the bed, Baby," he ordered, spotting the three-year-old Great Dane where he had no business being but always was when Derek wasn't looking.

The dog growled.

"And no back talk. Scoot. Now."

Grumbling and groaning, Baby unfolded his long limbs and obeyed. Without sparing Derek another look, clearly miffed, he lumbered out of the room.

"And stay out," Derek grumpily called after him. Damn dog, plunking himself right on top of my suit.

Derek tossed the towel aside, shook out the suit and tie he'd begun to shed the minute he walked in the door and hung them away. Then he stepped into some beat-up old sweats, an outfit much more in keeping with his inner self.

He liked his job, but detested the trappings. He had been raised in a simple home and his tastes had remained simple. Nor was owning the BMW a contradiction there. It, too, was simple, understated, comfortable and reliable.

All the things Derek valued; all the things Derek liked to think—hoped—that he himself was.

Driving was something he actually loathed, too. Aside from the shameful fact that he'd always been prone to car sickness, he much preferred a slower, more healthful mode of transportation. In winter he often went from his little farm to the store on his cross-country skis with Baby loping along beside him. And when the weather was good he bicycled to where he needed to go, again with the dog by his side. That way they both got fresh air and exercise, while going by car all they did was pollute the environment as their muscles turned to lard.

None of which he and Margo had ever been able to see eye-to-eye on, and he and B. J. Rawlings well might not, either. But whoa, boy—he was getting way ahead of himself. So far the lady hadn't even returned his call.

B.J. had left her briefcase in his car—he'd found it when he got home an hour ago and he'd telephoned her house immediately. A woman had informed him that B.J. was taking a bath. She had asked for his number and said her daughter would call him back.

So she lived with her mother.

Derek felt as if he were constructing a jigsaw puzzle named Bertha Joanne Rawlings. As little pieces of information were being handed to him here and there, he was able to ever so slowly put together a complete picture of her.

Strange, but until he kissed her, he hadn't realized how badly he wanted to know the whole of her. She had intrigued him, irritated him, attracted him before, but with that kiss she had bewitched him. Stirred him. Tantalized and caught him, making it clear to him that he couldn't possibly go through the rest of his life without knowing to the fullest the heat and the passion she so cleverly disguised behind a crisp business facade.

He had sensed it in her the night of the party, when she had been "Joanie." It had called to him then like a siren's song, and he had come....

Well, he was still coming. Even if she was no longer "Joanie," even if she professed horror and regret about the kiss they shared. Even if she was cold with him. He knew that coldness was a sham. Bertha Joanne Rawlings was one passionate woman, and she had responded to *him*.

The bedside phone warbled. Derek snatched up the receiver. "Yes?"

"It's B. J. Rawlings. I'm told you have my briefcase."

"Yes, I—"

"Thanks for letting me know where it is."

"You're welcome, but—"

"Just bring it to the office tomorrow, if you don't mind."

"Well sure—"

"Thank you, Mr. Coleman. Good night."

Damn!

Derek slammed down the phone. And then, still wound up as tight as a coil, slapped his hand against the wall for good measure. Hard. Damn, damn, *damn* the woman and her stiff neck! The wall shook and his palm stung.

Muttering curses, wiping his smarting hand along the side of his pants, he went to the chest of drawers, took out some socks and yanked them on. Then he stomped out of the bedroom and up the hall, grabbed a down jacket out of the closet and stepped into lined boots. He snatched his keys and *her* briefcase up off the sideboard and slammed out the door.

An affronted Baby raised hell behind him and was ignored. Derek stabbed at the knob that activated the garage door opener, got into his car and roared off into the night.

Physical labor always cured whatever ailed B.J. and so, as soon as eating dinner was out of the way, she announced to her startled mother that she would start on the spare bedroom they had been wanting to redecorate.

"You want to put up wallpaper now?" her mother gasped. "At seven o'clock at night?"

"Not put up, Mom. Take down."

"But you've just had a bath...."

"So I'll have another one later. Excuse me." B.J. brushed past her mother and ran down into the basement where her father's workbench and tools were located. She hunted up some scrapers and brushes, and whatever other paraphernalia she might conceivably need for the task of ridding the spare bedroom walls of layers of old paint and wallpaper.

Feeling as she did, all stirred up and wired as if from too much caffeine, that loathsome job was just what she needed to work off steam. Speaking of which...

"The steamer, Mom," she called up the stairs. "Is it down here?"

Though she had never actually taken off wallpaper before, it stood to reason that steaming the wall would make the old paper easier to remove. She was sure she'd seen her father do it, too.

"Should be."

B.J. hunted it up in a dusty corner. She swiped at some cobwebs and dragged the thing out. She was wearing a faded Huskies sweatshirt and roomy washed-out overalls, one of her favorite at-home outfits. Similar togs used to be her childhood and adolescent "uniform," symbols of her willingness to turn herself into the boy her father yearned for with such a futile and abiding longing. These days the scruffy outfits merely spelled comfort and practicality.

Up in the spare room she dragged all the portable pieces of furniture, knickknacks and pictures out into the hall. Her Grandmother Rawlings's old-fashioned poster bed and armoire, too heavy to move, she covered with sheets of plastic. She was working up a fine sweat and often stopped to wipe the perspiration off her brow.

She set up the steamer, climbed up the ladder with it, and let loose with a blast of steam. Except it wasn't steam that gushed from the nozzle, but water. It bounced off the wall, liberally dousing B.J. in the process, while another stream trickled steadily into her sleeve and down her raised arm.

"Damn, damn, *damn!*"

"My words exactly, about an hour ago."

"What?!" At the sound of Derek Coleman's baritone from behind her, B.J. twisted around, teetering on the ladder and spraying water everywhere. "Don't just stand there," she yelled over the rat-tat-tat of the machine's motor, too busy for shock. "Turn that monster off."

Derek blessedly complied with dispatch. Quiet reigned, and the flow from the nozzle was reduced to a trickle, which promptly joined the puddle that had already formed in the pit of B.J.'s raised arm. She lowered it and shivered as the moisture coldly wet the side of her torso.

"Grrrr," she muttered, teeth clenched. Feeling shell-shocked, she gingerly climbed down the ladder. At the bottom she turned to face Derek, and that was when it hit her—Derek Coleman, national sales manager of Morrison Erectors and her figurative boss; Derek Coleman, the man who not six hours ago had kissed her into a state of quivering jelly, was lounging in the doorway of *her* spare room and had witnessed her ineptitude.

"What are you doing here?" She could only stare at him, he looked so different. Ratty sweats and stocking feet. "Where are your shoes?"

Derek couldn't help it, he had to laugh. To see his oh so proper district sales manager half-drenched and with wisps of cobweb clinging to her silvery mane certainly made the drive over here worthwhile. To see her completely nonplussed and reduced to inane stammerings was an added bonus. And to witness her battle with that vintage steamer had been like having front-row seats at the "I Love Lucy" show.

"Well, I'm glad one of us is amused." B.J. dropped the steamer hose and would have stalked from the room had Derek's bulk not blocked the doorway. Trapped, she contented herself with crossing her arms across her chest, while with one foot impatiently tapping she waited for Derek's mirth to run its course. She could see it might take a while, since every time he looked at her, something set him off again.

Watching through narrowed eyes as he laughed, she was nevertheless struck anew by how different he was tonight, and how appealing. His hair was wild and curly, two elongated dimples bracketed his mouth and the well-worn gray sweats loosely but lovingly draped his lean, yet solid frame. Long legs were crossed at the ankles with one foot propped up on its big toe, while on the other foot its partner was sticking out of a king-size hole in the sock.

For reasons unknown, that hole, that naked toe, made B.J. want to cry. It seemed to say so much to her, that hole. It spoke of vulnerability, of being alone and of not always being able to cope. It tugged at her heart.

And that scared her to death.

She dropped her arms and raised her eyes, only to find Derek no longer laughing but instead studying her as intently as she had been studying him.

"You shouldn't have come," she whispered.

"Yes, I should." Derek pushed away from the doorjamb and approached her. His voice was low and gravelly, and all the while his eyes were locked on hers. "I brought your briefcase."

"I—" B.J. swallowed, and backed up a step. Her rump connected with the foot of Grandma Rawlings's bed. "You shouldn't have."

"I wanted to." Derek stood right in front of her now. He laid his hands on her shoulders. His proximity forced B.J. to tilt her head back so that she could look into his face. It was grave. "I wanted to apologize for taking advantage of the situation this afternoon in the car. You didn't give me the chance on the telephone and I didn't want to leave it till tomorrow. The office is no place to discuss things that are private between us."

"There are no private things between us," B.J. said weakly.

"Aren't there?"

"Only the..." Inadvertently her eyes dropped to Derek's lips, so very close. She swallowed nervously. "Only what happened this afternoon."

"A kiss happened this afternoon, B.J."

"One you've just apologized for."

"No." Derek gently touched the back of his hand to her cheek. "I apologized for taking advantage, not for the kiss. Never for the kiss."

He said the last in a whisper, his lips almost touching B.J.'s slightly parted ones as he spoke.

"Something pretty terrific happened between us this afternoon, Bertha Joanne. You do know that, don't you?"

Something pretty terrific was happening to her right now, B.J. thought.

"Hmm." For several fluttering heartbeats, B.J. hoped he would kiss her again. She felt her eyelids droop and her body sway toward him.

But Derek's grip on her shoulders tightened, keeping her where she was.

"No," he said softly. "Not here, not now. I told your mother I would only stay up here for a minute, and in any case I think it might be best if each of us gave some thought to where we want things to go from here, you and I."

"Y-you and I?"

"Yes, you and I." Derek released her. At the door he turned. "I'll be over Saturday morning at ten," he said, "to teach you a thing or two about steamers and stripping walls before you botch the job completely. *Ciao.*"

And with a wink and a smile he was gone.

Chapter Six

Before you botch the job completely.

It drove her crazy, and it was probably childish, but B.J. couldn't get Derek Coleman's parting shot out of her mind all night. And she awoke with the firm resolution that, come hell or high water, that spare bedroom would be newly wallpapered *without* benefit of that man's expertise, thank you very much.

The weather had taken a giant leap forward into spring and the expected thaw quickly accomplished what would have taken the city's maintenance crews quite a bit longer. B.J. and Derek's meeting with the Wanger executives had been rescheduled for eleven o'clock.

Derek comported himself as professionally as he ever had, and of course B.J. did no less. Every now and then, however, when their eyes chanced to meet, it seemed to B.J. there was laughter lurking in the depths of his and that his lips twitched as though he were remembering the steamer fiasco with amusement. She would grit her teeth then and think to herself, Well, just you wait, Mr. Know-it-all.

As soon as they left Wanger and parted company—divergent commitments had made them come in separate cars—B.J. headed for the nearest paint store. She asked to speak to an expert, and some forty minutes later walked out of the store armed with newly acquired wallpapering knowledge and a load of up-to-date supplies guaranteed to make the job of stripping and hanging a cinch.

As quickly as she could, she got another sales call and some office work out of the way, and after telling Cally "TGIF, and why don't you knock off early, too," B.J. hurried home.

Her mother was having a cup of tea when B.J. tottered in with a bag of stuff in each arm.

"What on earth?" She hurried to relieve B.J. of one of the bags, peering into the top of it.

"Paint supplies," B.J. answered her unfinished question, setting the remaining bag down on the kitchen table. "I'm just going to change my clothes and then I'm tackling that spare room again."

Her movements brisk and full of purpose, she shrugged out of her coat on her way up the stairs to her room. She put it into her mother's waiting hands. "I'm dying to get started."

"Get started?" Having hung up the coat, Bertie followed B.J. up the stairs, frowning. "That nice young man from your office told me last night he was coming over tomorrow at ten to help you with that. I invited him to have breakfast."

"You *what*?" B.J. froze in the act of stepping out of her suit skirt.

"Well, he did say he's a bachelor..."

What was her mother up to? A little matchmaking? She had better not be. B.J. searched her face for clues, saying, "Sooo?"

"So he's bound to appreciate some good home cooking." Bertie met her daughter's narrowed eyes without guile. "I thought I'd make my famous Swedish pancakes. Your father always used to love them."

"And I'm sure De—Mr. Coleman will love them, too." Satisfied that her mother's motives were pure, B.J. finished undressing. "Actually, it's just as well you invited him. That way, his coming over here won't have been a *complete* waste of his time."

Out of habit, Bertie began picking up B.J.'s discarded clothes and hung them up. B.J. would have eventually done it herself, of course, but not being the tidiest person who ever lived, it might have taken a day or two.

"Won't he be upset when he finds you've gone ahead and done the room without him, darling?"

"Maybe." Humming a snappy tune, B.J. pulled a sweatshirt over her head. This one bore the WSU Cougar logo. She was thinking that she would enjoy pushing some of Derek Coleman's macho assumptions back down his throat. Botch the job completely, would she? Ha!

"And didn't you say he was your boss?"

"Yup." Nimbly B.J. secured overall straps to overall bib, then braided her hair with equal dispatch. "But that's at work. This is private, and he has no right whatever to stick his nose where it's not wanted. The nerve of him anyway," she grumbled, some of last night's resentment kindling anew. "As if I'm not as capable as any man, any day of the week."

Her mother closed the closet door, her expression thoughtful. "So you're still on that kick, are you, love?"

B.J., tying the laces on her sneakers, looked up sharply. "What's that supposed to mean?"

Bertie shrugged. "I suppose I'd hoped you'd outgrown that stuff."

"That *stuff*, Mother?" B.J. stood, matching her mother's frown. "What stuff is that, exactly?"

"That stuff, that *nonsense*, your father filled your head with," Bertie exclaimed, in a rare display of temper. "You're a woman, B.J., and for heaven's sake, what's wrong with that?"

In the silence that followed, it would have been difficult to say which of the two women was more shocked by the uncharacteristic outburst. As the bedroom clock ticked off the seconds, they stood staring at each other.

"You're angry," B.J. stated at last, a note of surprise in her tone. "You're really, really angry."

"You bet I am." Bertie clasped B.J.'s hands, squeezing them for emphasis, as she said in a voice of gentle urgency, "Please, don't misunderstand, darling. I love you and I'm proud of who you are and all you've accomplished. I just wish you would be, too."

"You think I'm not?" B.J. asked incredulously. She withdrew her hands, paced a few steps, then faced her mother with an accusing look. "What are you really saying, Mother? That I'm not happy with who I am?"

Bertie sighed. "I'm saying you're smart, you're beautiful, you're successful—be proud of it and enjoy it." She reached for B.J.'s hands again. "I'm saying, your father's opinion to the contrary, it's not at all necessary to know everything, to be the best at everything. There's nothing wrong with needing help—"

"Pop used to say God helps those who help themselves, Mom." B.J. pulled her hands out of her mother's and marched out the door. "And you know something? He was right."

Down the stairs she went, Bertie right behind her. "Well, he wasn't right about everything."

"Right enough to suit me."

Her mother never *had* understood, B.J. fumed, recalling the many times Bertie had tried to contradict something her husband had said, or the times she had brought home dresses for B.J. and tried to convince her to wear them. Pop would laugh uproariously, and after a little nudging, B.J. would join in.

She used to hear her mother plead with her husband about the way their only child was being raised, but in the end, her father's way had always prevailed, and B.J. was glad.

So what if often she had ached to the bone from the rigorous regimens he had imposed on her in the course of her training? So what if she had had no friends besides Mandy, no dates? She had nearly made the Olympic ski team, hadn't she?

Pop was more fun and a better friend than any of the dumb kids at school would have been, anyway. He took her to shows and plays that had meaning, that taught something, as did the books they read and had such fun dissecting.

So who had needed the giggling, the whispered confidences and the slumber parties Mandy had sometimes participated in and told her about? She had had campouts with Pop under the stars, where she had spent hours finding and naming planets and constellations for him. They would discuss men such as Copernicus, Gauss and Schweitzer, men of science, men of vision, while the girls at school wasted their time with rock stars and movie idols.

Pop had torn to shreds the rock-star poster which had been a birthday present from Mandy, and which B.J. had tacked up on the inside door of her closet. She had cried....

Remembering, B.J. angrily shook her head. She had had a great childhood, a super adolescence.

She snatched the bags of supplies off the table and hugged them to her chest as if for protection against the unsettling memories that encroached on the good ones, which—gilded by time and repetition—offered comfort and answers to the whys and wherefores which sometimes plagued her. Turning to leave the kitchen, she saw her mother in the doorway, watching her with a quizzical expression.

B.J. tossed her head. "I loved Pop very much."

"I know you did." Bertie's smile was bittersweet. "I did, too. He was a wonderful man. But—" She shook her head.

"But what?" B.J. prompted, more curt than she normally was with her mother. She was chafing under what she perceived to be her mother's criticism of her and of the person who had shaped her most. And she was not too thrilled with herself for feeling defensive.

She returned her mother's troubled gaze with a frown, which darkened into a full-fledged scowl when Bertie quietly said, "But he wasn't God, B.J."

"I never thought he was."

"Didn't you? Don't you still?"

Did she?

Even as she stormed out of the kitchen, up the stairs and furiously set to work on the spare room, the question haunted B.J. Stirring up the mixture that would penetrate and loosen the old wallpaper, it nagged at her. Tearing the strips of paper off the wall, there it was. And the answer that persisted was always, No. She'd never thought him to be God. Pretty darn near, maybe...

He knew so much. He knew everything, she used to think. Especially he used to know when she wasn't really trying, or when she would inwardly rebel about something he thought she should do. Or when, as with that poster, she had disappointed him.

He would get this look on his face at those times, this look B.J. came to dread, to hate. A pitying sort of look, not contemptuous, not angry, just sort of... *pitying*.

It was a look that said to her, Poor thing. I guess you can't help being as inferior as you are.

He would say as much aloud, sometimes, too. "Poor baby," he'd say. "I keep forgetting that you're only a girl."

Almost viciously, B.J. tore strips of wallpaper off the wall. She was panting, from the exertion as well as from the feeling that a rope was relentlessly being tightened around her chest. Teeth gritted, she willed those memories away. Instead, she tried to do what she always did on those blessedly few occasions when they reared their ugly heads—to concentrate on the positive, the gilded ones. But this time they eluded her.

"This is a man's world." How he had pounded that pronouncement into her. "If you want a place in it, be respected in it, you'd better think like a man and work like a man. That means stand on your own two feet, B.J., don't lean on anyone, don't let 'em see your weaknesses."

As a consequence, she worked hard at hiding her weaknesses and uncertainties. Her major one had to do with precisely the stuff she had been mulling over just now, and boiled down to one thing—her identity. Lately it seemed she had been less and less happy with who she was. In fact, half the time she no longer even *knew* who she was. Her accomplishments had become less and less important; she no longer took joy in them as she once had.

More and more some secret, suppressed part of her fought to come to the surface. More and more, too, impressing Pop, making him proud, was no longer the name of the game.

When had it ceased to be?

And what was the name of this new game?

Wiping the sweat off her brow with the back of one rubber-gloved hand, and trying to flick the last sticky bit of wallpaper from the fingers of the other, B.J. stepped back to survey the bare walls.

Yuck.

That sound of distaste referred to the walls as much as to the uncomfortable reality of Derek Coleman having on several occasions been witness to, or even the instigator of the emergence of her suppressed inner self.

At Morrison's party, for instance—whatever female sense of whimsy had possessed her to misrepresent herself like that to him? To come on all coy and flirty?

And on the drive back from Seattle—she had chattered like a magpie about inner thoughts and feelings she had never shared with any man before. And Derek Coleman was not just any man, either. He was a man she worked with and needed to impress with sterling, nose-to-the-grindstone, no-nonsense attitudes.

Then there was that cuddling session in the car when they were stranded, and that kiss...

Heat that had nothing to do with exertion and everything to do with the memory of her reaction to—and enthusiastic participation in—that kiss had B.J. break out in a drenching sweat. She had been neither thinking nor acting like the professional she was supposed to be during that kiss. She had only been feeling.

Feeling like a woman.

For the first time in her life, she had felt gloriously, wondrously, passionately, but in retrospect distressingly female.

Distressingly, because if she wanted to be an equal in a man's world—in Derek Coleman's world—acting like a woman would never do. Distressingly, because if they hadn't kissed, if Coleman's perception of her as a colleague and an equal had not thus been altered, he would never have dreamed of coming here and telling her she would "botch the job" if he didn't help her.

A man would have bopped him in the nose for such a crack!

As she commenced to furiously scour the stripped walls with a wall-cleaning solution, and as she had on countless occasions in the course of her twenty-nine years, B.J. fervently wished she could be a man. No longer necessarily for keeps, mind you, but just long enough for her to have decked that troublesome Derek Coleman with a neat uppercut.

B.J.'s back was killing her, her hands were a disaster and her eyes burned from lack of sleep. But the spare room looked fantastic. Even in the light of day.

And even according to Bertie, who duly praised her daughter's handiwork but afterward went back downstairs with a sigh and a shake of the head.

B.J. pretended she didn't see or hear it, just as she pretended she didn't feel a knot of trepidation in the pit of her stomach. Derek Coleman had wanted to help. He would be here soon now, and he was bound to get angry....

So what? She had merely elected not to accept said help. Why should she feel uneasy about that? It was her house, her spare room. She had the right to wallpaper it, if and when she chose, didn't she? You bet she had. Just as she had the right to reject help with it, if and when she chose.

Come to that—*she* hadn't invited him to breakfast, either. So was there really any reason why she should even have to be here when he came? None at all.

The snow was almost gone, the sun was shining. Maybe she would just give good old Mandy a call and make arrangements to pick up the kids for that outing she'd promised them. True, they had tentatively planned it for next weekend, but she did have that present for Jessica and she was free today—

The doorbell. He was here. Damn.

B.J. knew a moment of panic, but quickly stifled it. She could still leave, of course, but he would probably think she was trying to avoid him. Which was ridiculous, but there you were.

To prove her utterly serene state of mind, she called "I'll get it," to her mother and raced down the stairs. She shouldn't have raced, she told herself seconds later, and pressed a hand to her chest to slow her suddenly runaway heartbeat.

On a deep breath, she tilted her chin and opened the door. "Good morning, Mr. Coleman."

"Good morning." *Mr. Coleman?* One of Derek's brows arched. Back to that, were they?

The other brow followed suit, when he got a good look at B.J. She looked stunning in a pair of gray wool slacks topped by a bright multicolored sweater, but she was hardly dressed for the job they intended to do today.

"I said I'd help," he quipped, letting his gaze travel the length of her more slowly and deliberately, so she would get the point, "not that I'd do all the work alone."

B.J. flushed. "Won't you come in," she said, avoiding his eyes by glancing at the bulging tote he carried.

"Tools of the trade," Derek answered her unspoken question. "I remodeled my own place not too long ago and still had most of the stuff we'll need today." Chuckling, he stepped past her into the house. "You can put that steamer thing of yours in the trash, I'll tell you that right now."

"I already did."

"Good. All right if I leave this here till later?" At her nod, he set the bag down, and briskly rubbing his hands, sniffed the air. "Something sure smells wonderful."

"Mother's fixing Swedish pancakes."

"Is she?"

B.J. nodded, moving past him to lead the way into the kitchen. Derek caught her arm and stopped her. "I was referring to you," he murmured, his eyes trapping hers. "To that tantalizing scent you always wear."

"Oh." At a loss as to how to deal with or respond to such a statement, B.J. could only stare helplessly back at him. Spellbound by his ardent gaze, she forgot all about being resentful, about being equal, about being a man and poking him in the nose.

She forgot everything but what Derek's eyes told her—that she was a woman, and that he thought her beautiful. Desirable.

Always, till now, B.J. had turned cold beneath similar glances—they had made her feel threatened, belittled, like an object instead of a person. She had expected to feel the same with Derek just now, but she didn't. Far from it.

She felt bathed by the warmth of his perusal; she soaked it up as drought-stricken earth soaks up the healing rain. And as she did she felt something relax deep inside her, felt something unfold, something she had never realized had been all tight and twisted.

It wasn't a physical thing, not an organ that had been pinched or a muscle that had cramped and was now relaxed. It was a *feeling,* a sense of letting go, and it spread like a golden flame from the core of her throughout her whole body. It lit her face with a smile that was warm and genuine.

Derek was stunned by the sweetness of it. It stole his breath away. It made his fingers tighten on her arm, made a catalog full of fantasies spring to life.

"You're beautiful," he whispered fervently, and was rewarded with a shaky sigh and a smile that suddenly wobbled.

"I used to hate being told that."

"And now...?"

B.J. flushed. But though her lids fluttered, she kept her gaze steady on his. "Now, from you, I— It's nice."

"*You're* nice," he said softly.

"How do you know?" B.J. asked with a breathless little laugh. "You don't really know me, not the real me."

"I'd like to, though." Derek moved so that they were chest to chest. He put his arms around her, loosely, without demand. "I'd like to very much." His eyes searched hers. "How do you feel about that, Ms. Rawlings?"

Scared to death.

As she hesitated to reply, her thoughts must have shown in her eyes, because Derek's began to sparkle with rueful amusement. They crinkled endearingly at the corners, as he said, "You know something? It scares me, too."

"This is all very startling and new to me," B.J. felt compelled to explain, lest he think her coy. "I'm not sure how to act."

"Unfortunately, it's not quite so new for me." Derek rubbed her back, urged her body closer. "I wish it were. I'd be less scared if it were."

"Once burned...?"

"Hmm." Derek scanned B.J.'s perfect features and felt the same jolt of reaction he had felt looking at her across Morrison's crowded living room. What was it? Not merely her beauty, of that he was sure. No, he mused, more likely it was that air of innocence she had, that hint of vulnerability, of uncertainty.

It's as if she were just a young girl, not yet sure of her femininity and a little afraid of its power.

Those qualities were totally absent from B. J. Rawlings, the professional woman he saw at the office almost every day, but they were very evident—at least to him—when B.J. shed that workday facade, as she had on their ski interlude, and a few days ago in his arms, after they had slid into the ditch.

There were times when the cynic in him, the man who had been married to a woman much like the public B.J., the ambitious and brilliant district sales manager, wondered if the vulnerability he found so intriguing was for real.

Was it possible for a woman to be smart, hard-driving and sophisticated, and still have this ingenue quality? Derek had promised himself to find out. And if he found B.J. to be the real thing, why then...

But that was for later. For now...

"Have dinner with me tonight, Bertha Joanne."

It was on her tongue to say, "Yes, I'd love to," when B.J.'s gaze chanced on the bag of tools on the floor and she remembered the spare room. Her heart sank. Oh, Lord, why hadn't she waited for his help? There was no way he would still want to spend time with her when he found out what she had done. The sense of loss she knew she would feel when he turned from her and left, already made her ache. All she could do was postpone the inevitable for as long as possible.

"If you still want to, later," she evaded, "then I'd like to very much."

Derek laughed. "Think I'll be too tired, is that it?"

"What's keeping the two of you?" Bertie stuck her head out into the hall.

Never had an interruption been more timely or more welcome. "We're just coming, Mom."

B.J. led the way to the kitchen, sending a small smile back across a shoulder to Derek as Bertie tut-tutted about keeping company standing in the hall when they had a perfectly good living room.

"I thought you might have taken Mr. Coleman upstairs already," Bertie said, pouring Derek some coffee after they were seated at the kitchen table.

"Not before he's had his breakfast, Mother," B.J. replied, with a glance of warning that earned her a disapproving one from her mother in return.

Derek, oblivious to such undercurrents, added sugar to his coffee and said, "Please, Mrs. Rawlings, call me Derek. Maybe if you do," he added, with a meaningful glance toward B.J., "your daughter will remember to do the same."

His teasing message wasn't lost on B.J. She had called him Mr. Coleman when he had arrived. How radically, and from her perspective startlingly, their relationship had been altered in the short span of time between then and now. As she smiled a little weakly in response to his gentle jibe, she couldn't help but wonder if after he had seen her handiwork upstairs they would be back to square one or worse.

The thought distressed her. To push it away, she picked up the platter of thin rolled-up pancakes and held it out to him. "Let's eat before these get cold."

"They look and smell wonderful." Derek helped himself to a healthy serving.

Bertie beamed. "Everyone tells me they taste good, too. Try the blackberry jelly on them. Homemade."

"Delicious."

When everyone had served themselves, they ate in silence for a few moments. Derek was enjoying every bite—B.J. might as well have been eating cardboard.

At the very least Derek would be taken aback, she was thinking miserably, and rightly so. Funny, how she hadn't thought of how he would feel before now or, more correctly, how she hadn't *cared* how he would feel. He'd been nice enough to offer his help. The very least she could have done was tell him, No, thanks, I'll manage.

Or she could have let him help.

Her gaze collided with her mother's accusing one, and she knew her mother's thinking paralleled her own. But instead of mentally conceding her the point, B.J. bristled. Her earlier arguments, forgotten while the heat of Derek's desirous glances and seductive words had worked their magic, now blessedly came rushing back.

Whatever else she was, whatever else she became, she would never be able to accept a man's presumption of being more capable than she. No man was, besides which it didn't do to appear needy. She liked Derek Coleman—there, she had admitted it—but she didn't, couldn't *need* him. If she did, she would be lost.

Chapter Seven

Muted blue stripes on a neutral background.

Derek decided he would have chosen similarly. She had done a good job of hanging the paper, too.

Well.

He stepped back a pace, disillusioned rather than angry and thinking that he had certainly been put in his place by the inimitable Ms. Rawlings. Margo couldn't have done better.

So was she happy, he wondered, now that she had finally sprung her little surprise on him? Was she chuckling to herself, standing there behind him statue-still? Taking his time, firmly banishing all expression from his face, he turned to face her.

B.J. wasn't laughing.

Grudgingly giving her credit for tact, he let his gaze meet hers—and what he saw went a long way toward soothing his wounded feelings. Not only was B.J. not laughing, her eyes were wide with apprehension and soft with... pleading? She was gnawing on her lower lip and twisting her fingers into knots.

On the whole, she looked like a kid who had done wrong and was waiting to be punished, and it was clear that whatever emotions had prompted her to pull this stunt, she regretted them now.

The knot in the pit of Derek's gut relaxed. In fact, as it dawned on him that she clearly expected him to be furious, a peculiar, tender sort of amusement made him want to smile. So that was why she had been so evasive about having dinner with him tonight, he thought—she was expecting him to see her handiwork, blow up and bow out.

Well, Ms. Rawlings, two can play the surprise game.

"Nice paper," he drawled, adding as he moved farther into the room, "if a bit boring for my taste."

Behind him, pent-up air was being expelled with an audible hiss. Good, Derek thought with satisfaction, he was getting the lady's dander up. Whistling soundlessly to himself, he went to examine the nearest wall more closely. With his finger he felt for seams his eyes were unable to detect. He couldn't feel any, either.

No doubt about it, she had done a helluva good job.

"Not bad," he commented, "considering. Lucky, too, that with a pattern like this a few bubbles and overlapping seams aren't too noticeable."

He was gratified to hear a definite gasp from behind him that time. "Bubbles!?" There was outrage in both syllables. "Let me see where!"

B.J. shouldered into place next to Derek and stuck her nose within an inch of the paper. "There are no bubbles." Her hands smoothed over the wall, making double sure. She spun to face him. "There are *no* bubbles, Derek Coleman."

"No?" Derek's brows arched. "I guess it must've been a lump on the wall underneath that I felt, then."

"There are no lumps on those walls, either."

Shrugging, he conceded, "Well, maybe you're right. So—" brows arched, he looked at her flushed face "—who'd you get to do the job, Ms. Rawlings? Pete Mason? I hear he does good work, though he's a little pricey. Joe Bascom, on the other hand—"

"*I* did the job."

For a moment Derek stared at her as though struck speechless with disbelief. Then he laughed. "Sure you did."

"I did," B.J. insisted hotly, and when he merely shook his head and laughed harder, frustration had her clenching her hands into fists. "I did, dammit. I *did*."

"Why?"

The softly voiced question was as unexpected as Derek's abrupt cessation of mirth. B.J. blinked as she struggled to shift gears. "What?"

"Why did you do it?"

Unable suddenly to look him in the eye, B.J. hung her head. "To prove to you I could," she said to the floor.

"To me?" Derek cupped her chin and gently forced it up. He waited until she raised her eyes, as well. "I never doubted that you could."

"But you said—"

"I was teasing. I was glad to have chanced upon an excuse to come over here again, and you were such a riot with that antique steamer gizmo..."

He chuckled, seeing her again in his mind's eye—disheveled and dripping and oh-so-adorable in her outrage with that recalcitrant hose and nozzle.

"Did you really want an excuse to come over here again?"

"What do you think?"

What did she think? Slowly B.J. smiled. It was a smile that grew out of the happiness she suddenly felt. "I think you're still teasing me, but I don't care." She bit her lip. "I'm sorry, Derek."

The apology and the sweet sound of his name on her lips seemed to Derek like a giant step in the very direction he wanted things between himself and B.J. Rawlings to go. Catching both of her hands in his, he pulled her toward him until their bent arms were snugly trapped between their chests.

"So now what?" he asked huskily. "I'm here, and there's nothing for me to do. It seems to me you owe me a day of activity."

"I do?"

"Uh-huh." His eyes on hers, he pressed a kiss on the knuckles of her hand. "I could come up with some mutually rewarding pastimes, but something tells me you might think that a mite too soon." His lips moved to tantalize the knuckles of her other hand. "Or would you?"

B.J.'s eyes got tangled up in his, and unused to flirtatious banter and already breathless from their belly-to-belly proximity, she gave a shaky little laugh. "I would."

He gave a comically exaggerated sigh of regret. "I was afraid of that. Your turn."

B.J. shook her head. "I—I can't think, with us standing like this."

"Good." Derek's grin was practically oozing male satisfaction, but for once B.J. didn't mind. As he let go of her hands and stepped back, she was busy coming to grips with the realization that the relief she felt at having her hands released and his body removed was liberally tinged with regret.

"I, uh, I'd kind of been thinking of driving out to Mandy's and getting the kids," she said. "I owe Jessie her birthday present..." She hesitated, mentally looking one more time before she leaped. "You could come with me if you'd like."

"Hmm. I would like, but—" Derek glanced at his watch "—since you mentioned birthday presents, I just remembered I still owe a certain little boy one of those. I gave part of his to Jessica, if you'll recall."

"The book. I wondered..."

"Yes, well, I have this Little Brother." Seeing B.J.'s questioning look, he elaborated, "Not the sibling kind of little brother, though I have one of those, too. He's twenty-two, lives in San Francisco and is a little old for a book called *Come See the Animals*, unless it pertains to a rock group. No, Justin Andrews is a ten-year-old who's being raised by a single mother in less than affluent circumstances. I participate in the Big Brother program..."

"You do? But that's wonderful."

"Yeah, well..." Praise like that embarrassed Derek. "Where are you planning to take the Jenks kids?"

"I noticed there's an animated movie playing at the cinema on Sparks Street."

"What say I meet you there? With Justin if he can, and otherwise alone?"

Her heart leaping, B.J. said "Great."

"Just the person I've been dying to see," was how Mandy greeted B.J. at the door. Earlier, Ron had answered the phone when B.J. called to announce her impending visit and plans with the kids. Now, as Mandy hustled her into the kitchen and with neither the kids nor

Ron in sight or even within hearing, B.J. wondered if she wouldn't have been smarter to stay away.

Ron had witnessed part of that kiss she had shared with Derek in the car. No doubt, he had wasted no time in telling Mandy, who was now panting for details!

She pushed B.J. into a chair, slammed a mug of coffee in front of her and then took the chair on the opposite side of the table. "Well?"

Not so fast, girl. Smiling, B.J. took a leisurely sip of coffee, looking her friend in the eye across the rim of the mug. "So, where are the kids?"

"Gone with Ron to the store." Mandy wiggled impatiently in her seat. "Tell me everything."

Conjuring up a puzzled frown, B.J. set down the cup. "Tell you everything about what?"

"All right, I get it." Mandy straightened, eyes narrowed. "You think I should mind my own business, right?"

"That would be refreshing, yes."

"Well I won't, so quit stalling. He kissed you," Mandy prompted, and with a glare added, "And don't you dare say, who."

"I wouldn't dream of it." B.J frowned. "But I will say this—your husband has a big mouth."

Mandy rolled her eyes. "Tell me something I don't know. Like what's going on with you and the hunk?"

The *hunk?* B.J. thought about the description, and an inward smile easing her frown, decided it fit. Aloud, however, she grumbled, "Isn't there some code of ethics tow-truckers have to abide by, for heaven's sake?"

"Nuh-uh. You're thinking of doctors and priests," Mandy told her. "Tow-truck drivers blab, and Ron more than most. Especially when he catches a certain friend of mine in a clinch with Jessica's heartthrob."

"Jessica's *heartthrob?*"

"Yup. Love at first present."

"Well, I'll be..."

"Like godmother, like goddaughter," Mandy pronounced with a wiggle of the brows. "So tell me, already."

"There's nothing to tell. We were—" B.J. struggled to sound offhand. "We were...sharing body heat, that's all."

For an instant Mandy gaped at her, and then she hooted.

Flushing, B.J. insisted "Well, it's true," but grinned when her eyes met Mandy's merry ones. "Or anyway that's how it started."

"Oh, B.J." No longer laughing, Mandy gripped her friend's hands. "I like him."

"I do, too," B.J. admitted.

"I'm glad." They looked at each other and shared a moment of silent communication. They had known each other a long time, had watched each other grow up and mature. B.J. had been there to see Amanda find true love and happiness with Ron, and Mandy had never made a secret of the fact that she wished a similar good fortune for B.J.

At length, she squeezed B.J.'s hands and released them. "A word of advice?"

B.J. grimaced. "Would it matter if I said I didn't want it?"

"No." Mandy got up and walked to the sink. For a moment she busied herself there and then abruptly she turned and said, "Do yourself a favor, girl—don't blow it."

Don't blow it.

Whatever "it" was, B.J. promised herself to give it a

shot. It might be nice to have a bit of romance in her life for a change. What could be the harm, as long as she kept it in perspective, as long as she didn't let it take over her life?

Derek Coleman was an attractive, exciting man. Even sitting in a darkened movie theater with three spellbound children putting a respectable distance between his seat and her own, B.J. was acutely aware of him. Every now and then she would feel his eyes on her like a physical touch, and a few times, when she turned her head and looked at him, too, their gazes had met and locked. Her mind had gone blank at those times—her heart had tripped over itself and her insides had turned to quivering tapioca.

Lust.

It was one of those words that conjured up images of steamy nights, naked bodies and black satin sheets. And it was a feeling that B.J. now knew she had never before experienced.

Ego not *Eros* had propelled her into Mark Quentin's arms seven years earlier.

Mark had been the golden boy at the engineering firm where they had both worked, his attentions had flattered her. She had fancied herself in love, but hadn't really been, of course. There had been no sense of loss when they had parted.

"In love" was not what she was with Derek Coleman, either, B.J. reminded herself. Nor was she going to be. The nice thing about maturity was that it allowed a person to enter into a sexual relationship without having to give lip service to such words as "love" and "ever after."

I want Derek Coleman's body, not his heart.

Maturity or not, admitting it—even just inwardly and to herself—had B.J. blushing. She shot Derek a quick glance. Thank God, he was looking straight ahead at the screen. She would die if he knew what she was thinking.

Derek felt B.J.'s glance but didn't dare look at her. He was afraid his eyes would betray the desire which had grown in leaps and bounds in the course of their occasional, lingering eye contact. In his mind he already had her in his bed, stripped and willing and preferably as soon as tonight. The fact that he knew tonight was out of the question—Justin was sleeping over—did nothing to cool his ardor. It merely made him promise himself that it would be soon. Real soon.

Wrapped up as they were in their separate, but similar musings and fantasies, the movie's end caught both B.J. and Derek by surprise. As the largely pint-sized audience clapped their hands and with high-pitched excitement recounted the show's high points to each other, the two of them returned to reality with guilty starts.

"Cute show, wasn't it?" B.J. said with false enthusiasm.

"Just darling." Derek's tone was dry as dust, as was the look he shot her as he got out of his seat. "Which was why we sat entranced long after it was over, right?"

Rising, too, B.J. reflexively felt a defensive retort coming on, but the wry twinkle in Derek's eyes disarmed her. "Right," she agreed with a chagrined little chuckle.

"Listen up, troops." Derek took charge of the children. "Follow Aunt B.J. out of the theatre. Single file."

"Can we have hot dogs, Aunt B.J.?" Jessica pleaded.

"Well, actually—"

"No way." This from Michael. "We had hot dogs last time. I want to have pizza, Aunt B.J. Can we, huh?"

Both children were not only *not* single filing, they were tugging impatiently on B.J.'s down jacket, blocking the aisle and creating a traffic jam.

B.J. was looking down at them helplessly. "Well, the thing is—"

"Please, Aunt B.J., hot dogs. Pleasepleaseplease."

"Well, really, darling, your mother said..."

B.J.'s ineffectual objection trailed away in surprise as Derek willy-nilly scooped Jessie up under one arm, collared Mikey with the other hand and with Justin hanging onto his coattail briskly marched up the aisle. She caught up with them in the lobby.

As soon as she saw B.J., Jessie started up about treats again. "Can we have ice cream, Aunt B.J.?"

"I want pizza!"

"Well, children, Mommy told me—"

"Popcorn. Can we have popcorn, huh? Please?"

"But you already had—"

"Hold it!" With a face like a thundercloud, Derek issued the command. Instant silence ensued. "The word from your mother was only one treat, which you already had, so that's the end of that. And she wants you straight home for supper at your Grandma's. Got that?"

"Yeth," Jessica lisped through the gap in her teeth.

Mikey pulled a face and nodded.

"I didn't hear you, Mike," Derek said.

"Yes, sir."

"Great." Derek clapped him on the shoulder and gave him a squeeze while sending a smile and a wink down to Jessica. "So let's say thanks to your Auntie B.J. and go on home."

"Thank you, Aunt B.J.," the Jenks children obediently chorused.

"Y-you're very welcome," B.J. replied in a daze, her eyes asking Derek, How do you do that?

"Where did you learn to do that?" B.J. asked Derek later, after the Jenks children had been dropped off and the two of them and Justin were headed back to B.J.'s car which they had left at the theatre. She would get in it there and follow Derek out to his house. He had invited her to dinner, and knowing Justin would act as chaperon, B.J. hadn't hesitated to accept.

Lust and all it entailed had been great to contemplate in the darkened movie house. Once back in daylight, however, her inbred inhibitions had asserted themselves and a chaperon—even a ten-year-old one—would be very welcome. Actually, Derek had invited B.J.'s mother, as well—surely a sign that his intentions were strictly honorable—but Bertie was having her monthly bridge group over and had declined.

"Those kids usually manage to walk all over me," B.J. elaborated. "Why is that?"

"They know you're a pushover."

"Well, I want them to like me...."

"They liked me well enough, don't you think?" Derek took his eyes off the road long enough to slant her a warm glance. "Even though I don't put up with their guff."

"Hmm." When Derek looked at her like that, it was difficult to remember what they were discussing. How could she ever have thought him a stuffed shirt? "So, uh—as I said...where'd you learn all that? I mean, you don't have any of your own. And Justin—" B.J. smiled at Justin contentedly listening to Derek's portable radio in the back seat. "He's such a well-mannered little guy, I can't imagine him ever giving you a lick of trouble."

"Ha." Derek tossed his head, remembering. "A year or so ago when I first started spending time with him, a mouthier, more obnoxious little jerk never walked the streets. We've since come to an understanding."

He said it so mildly, B.J. chuckled. "What'd you do, trounce him?"

"I'd never do that." Derek's quick sideways glance was wry. "That's not to say there weren't times when I was sorely tempted. No, what I did was simple—I gave the boy choices. If you do this, then that will follow. If you choose to do something else, then so-and-so will happen. He's a smart kid, he learned pretty fast to make the right kind of choices."

Choices. B.J. wondered what hers might have been, if her father had allowed her the freedom to make them. "You'd make a wonderful father," she told Derek softly, at length.

"I'd like to be one, that's for sure."

"Then you want to get married again?" Why should the thought of Derek marrying cause her chest to constrict the way it was doing?

"It's crossed my mind, yes." His voice dropped an octave, becoming intimate. "Would you care to be a candidate, Ms. Rawlings?"

"H-hardly." B.J.'s laugh was a trifle hollow, to her own ears, at least. "I'll let someone else be the mother of your children, thank you very much."

"Pity." Derek said it flippantly, had intended to mean it that way, too. But B.J.'s flat refusal of his backhanded proposal had ended his good humor. He was glad to see her car up ahead.

B.J. was also relieved to get off on her own for a bit. All her values, all her goals and accepted limitations seemed like bars on a cage whenever she spent any nonbusiness-related time in Derek Coleman's company. He made her want to bend the rules she had made for herself, made her want to break them. He made her wish it were possible to become something, some*one* she knew she could never be.

After getting out of his car she hesitated, beset by second thoughts. Maybe going to his house, becoming more closely acquainted and possibly involved wasn't such a good idea after all. "About dinner..." she hedged.

"Yes?"

"Perhaps it would be better if I didn't—"

"Why the hell not?" Derek interrupted testily.

Stung, B.J. straightened away from the window.

"I'm sorry." *Jeez, Coleman, get a grip.* Derek rubbed a hand across his face. "Look, if you'd really rather not..."

He looked so chagrined, B.J. relented. "Well, I *had* looked forward to seeing your home...."

Their eyes met. One of Derek's brows arched. "Is that all?" His intense gaze dared her to deny there was nothing more.

B.J. felt heat rush into her cheeks. She found it impossible to look away, but managed an innocent expression. "Steaks were mentioned, as I recall..."

Their eyes clung a moment longer and then Derek slowly smiled. "So they were." He put his car in gear. "Very well, Ms. Rawlings, get in your chariot and follow me. My home and your steak await...."

Derek lived quite a ways northward out of the city, in the direction of Colville and the Canadian border. It was pretty country out there, woodsy, with gently rolling hills and a little lake not far from his house. All the properties were at least several acres in size and many had horse paddocks or pastures in which animals grazed.

It would be a wonderful place to raise a family, B.J. thought, pulling into the spot at which Derek was pointing, next to the garage. Their earlier conversation had stayed with her all the way out to his place and she had caught herself a couple of times wondering what it would be like to have a baby. Derek's baby.

The image brought with it a feeling of bittersweet longing, a feeling that was not an entirely new one. Only now it seemed to have increased a thousandfold.

Shaking off the mood, telling herself to stop rattling cage bars, she hurried to catch up with Derek and Justin, who already were at the front door.

"I like your place," she told Derek. He was unlocking the door. "How many acres—"

The rest of her question turned into a shriek of terror as a huge animal leaped out the open front door, its slobbering tongue flapping, and headed straight for B.J. Before the second scream gathering in her throat could find release, two massive paws had clamped down on her shoulders, a blast of fishy breath was assaulting her nostrils and the lolling tongue wetly slapped at her face. Slowly B.J.'s legs buckled from a combination of fear and the animal's weight.

And that was all she knew.

She came to because something soft and wet was still brushing across her face. That tongue... The second scream she hadn't been able to get out earlier now made its belated exit from her throat. The wet thing was abruptly withdrawn. Her eyes popped open—and looked wildly into Derek's concerned ones. Peripherally she saw a washcloth in his hand. He had been washing her face.

With that reassurance, B.J.'s mouth clamped shut and she subsided back against the cushy piece of furniture she had been deposited on. All she cared about just then was that she wasn't on the ground with that... *thing* mangling her anymore.

"Are you all right?" Concern lent urgency to Derek's voice. "Are you hurt anywhere?"

Was she hurt? B.J. closed her eyes and listened to her body. "No."

She opened her eyes again and froze as they lighted on the beast that had attacked her. It lay on the carpet behind Derek and seemed about to devour Justin. One of its gigantic paws was draped across the little boy's chest and it was licking his face with the same gleeful concentration with which a child licks at the icing of a piece of cake before taking the first bite.

Horrified, B.J. pointed a shaking finger. "D-D-Derek," she croaked, another scream building as the creature opened wide its massive jaws, exposing gruesome fangs.

Derek looked where she pointed. "Good dog," he said. "Stay."

Turning back to B.J., he caught her still pointing finger along with the rest of her hand in the warmth of his and gently patted it. "That's Baby," he told her in a soothing tone. "I'm sorry he came at you the way he did, but believe it or not it means he likes you."

"L-likes m-me?" Sweet mercy, what did the thing do with people he didn't like?

"You bet." Derek looked and sounded pleased. Had the man gone insane? "Up until now, Justin and I were the only two people he greeted so affectionately." He grinned down at her. "You're a dog person, my girl. Baby can always tell."

A dog person? She? With a sound that was part laughter, part groan, B.J. struggled to sit up. Her mother's asthma made it impossible to have any kind of pet around, so all her life she had been petrified of dogs. All dogs, even toy poodles, for heaven's sake.

Behind Derek, Baby must have sensed B.J.'s movements. He stopped washing the now wildly giggling Justin's face, and ears pricking, looked up. His tail slapped the carpet.

Fascinated, B.J. stared at him, and gradually some sort of recognition dawned. "Why, it's...it's Marmaduke," she exclaimed. She had loved that cartoon in her youth.

"Baby's a Great Dane, yes." Derek's face and tone reflected paternal pride. "You'll find he's a very good boy."

"Baby?" B.J. stared at the beast—she could swear it—*he*—was actually smiling at her. She estimated its weight at two hundred pounds.

"Baby?" she repeated, incredulously. All at once, mirth bubbled up. She fell back on what she had since figured out was a couch covered in butter-soft leather and slowly began to laugh. "I don't believe it," she spluttered. "I don't believe any of this is really happening."

For the first time in his company, B.J. laughed with complete abandon. Watching, Derek's heart almost painfully contracted before it expanded wide, wide, wider. Something warm first trickled, then rushed like a raging river through his bloodstream and eddied in a fiery pool at the core of him.

Man, but this woman was something! Beautiful, smart, sexy. Now cool as mint, now warm as the sun. And never, *never* boring.

He wanted her.

"Bertha Joanne." He touched her face, her laughter stilled, as in a voice husky with emotion, Derek said, "Believe it, sweetheart. It really is happening."

Her eyes got lost in his hazel ones, now gleaming with the smoldering fires of tightly leashed passion. And she knew something was happening—had happened, to him and to her. Something momentous. Something life-altering. Something she hadn't wanted and for which she wasn't ready. Could never be ready.

Panicked, she bolted upright, swung her legs off the couch and stood. "I've got to go." She raked a trembling hand through her hair and looked everywhere but at Derek. "Where are my keys? Where's my bag?"

"What's gotten into you?" Derek, too, was on his feet. He tried to catch her hand, her arm, anything to hold her, but she jerked out of reach.

"Dammit, I want my keys." B.J. could feel hysteria coming on and tried to pull herself together. She saw Justin hug and soothe the dog, who had also stood up and was eyeing her with his head tilted to the side.

Everything, *everyone* in this room seemed determined to tug at her heartstrings. She had to get out of there!

She whirled as Derek touched her. "Please," she started, "I want my...! Oh."

She took the purse he handed her, and clutching it in both hands, took a couple of backward steps toward the door. "Well," she said, at a loss as to how to get out of the situation with her dignity intact, and then realized that she probably had none left, anyway.

She glanced at Justin, who looked back at her with world-weary eyes, as if he had witnessed similar confrontations all too many times. She could have cried, then.

"I'm sorry," she said to the room at large. "I'm really very sorry."

And then she turned and ran.

Chapter Eight

The fact that B.J. spent all day Sunday wallpapering her bedroom was a good indication of her distressed emotional state. As Bertie stood helplessly by, wringing her hands, B.J. made like a veritable whirling dervish, barely stopping for a cup of coffee, never mind food, and refusing to discuss what ailed her.

The reason for B.J.'s distress? Simple. She had committed the very sin she had sworn she wouldn't commit: she had let her heart get in the way of her common sense. *Lust,* she railed, as she stripped, scoured and pasted, was the only emotion she had given herself permission to feel for Derek Coleman. Why, she had even looked forward to indulging in a satisfying bout of it with him.

The other, the much more scary "L" word was not supposed to have entered the picture at all. But somehow it had.

And it had ruined everything.

How, she asked herself, could she possibly have a strictly sexual relationship, an affair, with a man she *loved?* She couldn't! It was out of the question. Apart from the fact that she would almost certainly be setting herself up for future heartaches, she just wasn't made that way.

Sure, Derek cared for her. That soul-destroying look of his, those velvet-voiced words that had had her tripping over herself in her haste to find the door out of his house had left her with no doubts about his feelings. Derek, too, had gone beyond mere sexual desire.

She would bet, however, that he, too, was spending his Sunday wallpapering or some such because of it. After all, the teasing remark he'd made in the car about her applying for the job of wife had surely been only that—teasing. But even if he had been serious, her reply would have been the same. Marriage, *children,* just weren't in her future.

So. Where did they go from here? was one of the questions that plagued B.J. as she attacked the walls of her room. Where was there left to go? was another.

But when she collapsed into bed that night, emotionally and physically exhausted, her last question was the one that had lurked at the back of her mind the entire day—*After the way I ran from his house, how in the world am I going to face Derek Coleman at the staff meeting tomorrow?*

She resolved not to for as long as possible. And to make sure he found no pleasure in looking at her—in the unlikely event he would even want to—she dressed for work in her most severe suit. Her hair was ruthlessly slicked back and secured in a spinsterish topknot. Her silk shirt was buttoned to the top, the shoes she wore were low-heeled and sensible. Horn-rimmed glasses took the place of her usual contact lenses.

The mirror told B.J. she looked terrible.

God, she looked beautiful, Derek thought, his eyes flying to B.J. like homing pigeons to their coop as he walked into the Monday morning staff meeting. He, on the other hand, felt—and no doubt looked—like hell.

He'd had a lousy Sunday, though he had made every effort to show Justin a good time. They had hiked some; they had taken the boat out on the lake and held poles in the water but, of course, they hadn't caught anything. They had picnicked, and then he'd driven the boy home.

Home. Now there was a laugh. A ramshackle walk-up on the wrong side of town, furnished in early junk shop. The place was perpetually in need of, but was rarely treated to the business side of a soapy mop.

Justin Andrews's mother, Starburst by name, had greeted them in a threadbare cotton kimono, which exposed more of her curvaceous body than it covered. She called herself an exotic dancer, which Derek privately translated to mean "stripper." She worked most nights and slept days. Saturday nights were particularly long for her, which was why Derek had Justin spend them with him as often as possible.

Starburst was only twenty-six, and from a distance, still lovely. Up close, however, and without aid of cosmetics, she looked a very tired forty.

As always, she had brightened at the sight of her son. That she loved the boy was obvious and one of the reasons Derek liked and respected her as much as he did. The other reasons had to do with the fact that, though she had barely completed eighth grade herself, she was determined to see Justin get a decent education. Starburst—

Lord only knew what her real name was—might be unschooled, but she didn't lack intelligence, and so she made sure Justin took advantage of all the breaks the social system provided.

Signing him up for the Big Brother program had been one of the ways in which she had tried to give her son a chance at something better. Another was hinting to Derek that, should he be interested, she might not be averse to giving Justin up to him for adoption.

The notion was tempting and Derek had thought long and hard before declining. Given his job and the travel requirements that went with it, in addition to his unmarried state, he hadn't felt qualified to accept the awesome responsibility of raising the boy. But he had lined up a tutor for Justin and had bought him a computer so that he could practice at home the things Derek taught him. Derek also helped with clothing and other expenses, though he would bite off his tongue before he ever mentioned those things to anyone else. Being allowed to witness and be a part of Justin's gradual transformation from pint-sized hooligan to an affectionate, no more than normally rambunctious preadolescent was all the reward Derek sought.

The boy filled a void in Derek's life, no doubt about it. He enjoyed sharing with Justin the talks and activities his father had shared with him.

Usually. Yesterday there had been no joy for him in their time together, because he couldn't get away from the fact that just when he realized that he had begun to care for Bertha Joanne Rawlings—wham, she'd slammed the door in his face.

He had stewed about B.J.'s headlong flight from him through two nights and one miserable day, and in the end he had decided what was needed was for him to back off.

B.J. cared for him, Derek was sure of it. In fact, he would bet his favorite fishing pole she felt plenty of the same things for him that he felt for her. All he needed to do was give her some space, let her get used to the idea a bit.

A week or two, a month at most, ought to do it.

First, however, they had this staff meeting to get through. Derek could see by the way she avoided his eyes that B.J. felt self-conscious this morning. He took pains to put her at ease.

"Good morning." He carefully kept his tone just cordial enough to let her know he wasn't upset with her, but not so cordial she might feel threatened again. He sat down in the chair next to hers—his customary seat at these meetings. "Remind me later to give the Wanger proposal back to you. We ought to have a good chance there, don't you think?"

"Hmm, yes. Definitely." B.J. busied herself with polishing her glasses. She told herself that Derek's businesslike demeanor relieved her, but the truth was it hurt to know he could take the Saturday night incident in stride like this. Had she read him wrong? Was it possible he didn't care?

The quick sideways glance she slanted him was met by a neutral smile. "Taking one of our engineers to the meeting with us was a stroke of genius on our part, too," he said, going on with his rehash of the meeting they had had last Friday.

The meeting from which B.J. remembered rushing more or less straight to the paint store. The meeting after which she had papered the spare room and thus set in motion the chain of events which had led her—them—to... this.

"Damn."

It was the sudden hush that brought home to B.J. the fact that she had uttered the epithet aloud. Every eye in the room swung toward her, including Floyd Morrison's. Floyd was standing, ready to call the meeting to order.

Scalding heat suffused B.J.'s entire body and she knew her embarrassment showed tellingly on her face. "I'm sorry, I—" She coughed into her fist, frantically searched for a plausible explanation. "I, uh, I just snagged my hose," she finally managed. "Six-fifty, shot."

To her relief everyone proceeded to exchange indulgent male glances, and they chuckled when Floyd told her. "Put it on the expense account, B.J. Cost o' doing business, don't you know?"

After which they got on with the business at hand, each department reporting on its respective area of responsibility. Derek and B.J. gave reports on active sales prospects, as well as on future projects for which the firm might want to submit bids. The meeting wound down with the usual announcements of general interest, such as charity contributions, changes in medical coverage and so forth.

"Before I call for a motion to adjourn," Floyd said at the end of the hour, "Jack Carruthers wants to say a few words about the company's mountaineering club. Jack."

"Thanks." Jack looked a little uncomfortable. Standing in front of a group of his managers obviously cramped his usually gregarious style. He got right down to business. "There's only a couple of you in this room who participate in the Mountaineers, but we'd appreciate it if the rest of you gentlemen—and lady—would get the word out to your staff. We'll be getting bulletins up later...."

"Excuse me, Jack." Derek raised a hand. "I think you need to give a pitch to a potential new Mountaineer member here." He let his hand drop onto B.J.'s shoulder. "Ms. Rawlings tells me she's a veteran climber. In fact, she and her father scaled Mount Rainier when she was only sixteen."

Listening, B.J. stiffened. What was Derek doing, bringing that up? She had been aware that the company had a mountaineering club, but had purposely kept her own climbing experience to herself. She didn't want to join. She hadn't tackled as much as a molehill since her father died.

But how could she refuse membership, now that Derek had spoken? He was bound to think she had made the whole thing up if she did. On the other hand, wasn't this a case of damned if she did and damned if she didn't? Of unpleasant consequences either way? So why not just say, Thanks, but I'm not into climbing these days?

She knew why she wouldn't say that, of course—because it would give the world—Derek Coleman—yet another glimpse of the flawed creature who huddled inside her supposedly beautiful and ultracompetent facade.

She mustered a smile. All around her people looked impressed. Derek preened, acting as proud as if she were his own creation, and Jack Carruthers eyed her with increased respect.

Floyd Morrison said, "I knew B. J. Rawlings would be a credit to our organization the minute I first clapped eyes on her in Denver."

As he went on to close the meeting, B.J. knew with a sick feeling in the pit of her stomach—a harbinger of things to come once she got up the mountain—that she was well and truly trapped.

She promised Jack Carruthers she would see him in a bit, and wanting nothing so much as a few quiet moments to herself, headed for the rest room. Derek caught up with her in the hall.

"B.J., I'd like a quick word with you."

"Can't it wait?"

"It'll only take a minute."

"All right." Bracing herself, B.J. followed Derek into his office. She stayed right by the door. "What can I do for you?"

"Now, there's a question." Derek's smile was gently rueful. He stood about a foot in front of her, but though he ached to reach out and smooth away the frown which was B.J.'s response to his teasing words, he kept his hands to himself. Stuffed them into his trouser pockets, in fact.

"I'm sorry." He nodded toward the chair by his desk. "Please sit a moment."

"I—" B.J. drew a deep breath, her frown increasing. "If you don't mind, I'd rather not. I'm leaving for Boise after lunch—"

"Oh, that's right. The Chalmers bid."

"Among other things. I'll be gone all week, and I've got a ton of stuff to do before I leave...."

"All right, I'll say this quickly." In spite of his resolution to the contrary, Derek touched her. He put one hand on B.J.'s shoulder.

His touch, a gentle kneading of his fingers into stress-tightened muscles, had B.J.'s knees go weak. How nice it would be to lean into Derek and have him hold her a while. To tell him the things that troubled her and have him say it was all right. But she knew she couldn't do that, just as she knew his response would probably have been a bracing shake and a hearty, Mind over matter, B.J.—just as her father's had always been.

She locked her knees and tried to shrug off Derek's hand. But he held tight.

"Things got a little crazy last Saturday night," he said, "and I wanted to apologize for that." When she would have spoken, he laid a finger across her lips. "Please, let me finish. I'd like us to be friends, B.J." He caught her gaze and held it. "Just friends. Two people who get together to talk, maybe share a meal or a movie, go hiking, whatever. I get lonely, B.J. Don't you?"

Trapped as she was by his gaze, B.J. knew only a truthful reply would do. And so, after a charged exchange of long and silent glances that left her trembling and not at all in mind of "just friendship," she whispered a choked, "Yes."

"Then can I call you on the weekend? Maybe see you?"

B.J. swallowed, and closed her eyes to shut out the searching intensity of his. She should stay away from him—she should say no. But wordlessly she nodded, Yes.

B.J. was on the road the rest of the week, and when she got home late Friday night Bertie had several things to tell her. The first was that Derek had called to let B.J. know there had been a family emergency—his father had suffered a slight heart attack. Derek would be in Seattle to be with his mother until his Dad was out of the woods. If B.J. had time, would she touch base with Justin this Saturday?

Bertie handed her daughter a slip of paper with the boy's address and phone number. The name and phone number of the kennel where Baby was boarded was also written on it. Further, he had said to tell B.J. that the spare key to his house was hanging from a nail beneath the back porch.

B.J. listened to it all with a whole potpourri of emotions, which included concern, sympathy and dismay, an equal dose each of disappointment and relief, as well as exhilaration at Derek's obvious faith and trust in her. Of course she would get in touch with Justin tomorrow and possibly even take him out somewhere if he liked. Perhaps the Cheney Cowles museum, or maybe they could ice skate at Riverfront Park.

Bertie's second item concerned herself. She had had her regular visit with Doc Lehmann that week and he had told her that what with it being spring and all manner of pollen messing up the air, his advice to her was: Get out of town for a couple of months. Arizona or New Mexico, take your pick, he'd said, handing her some brochures on residences with medical supervision to take home.

B.J. laid down the fork with which she'd been pushing her warmed-up supper around on her plate. What little appetite she'd had to begin with had fled long ago.

"So." She propped her elbows on the table, and with her hands folded beneath her chin, eyed her mother. "Which'll it be, Mom. Arizona or New Mexico?"

"What?" Bertie blinked. "Why, darling, neither, of course. You know, as well I do, we can't afford the sort of thing he suggests. I'll just stay indoors more, that's all."

"You'll do nothing of the kind." B.J.'s tone brooked no argument. She slapped her palms on the table and stood. "Tomorrow we'll make all the arrangements and do whatever clothes shopping we need to do. And on Sunday, my good woman—" B.J. stopped to give her mother an affectionate hug "—we're going to put you and your asthma on a plane heading south."

"B-but the money..."

"Is not an object," B.J. said firmly. "I came back here to work for Morrison to make sure it wouldn't be. Now, how about we go through your closet and..."

Mindful of Derek's request regarding Justin Andrews, B.J. telephoned the boy Saturday morning. She asked if he would like to go downtown shopping with her and her mother, but not surprisingly he declined. He was, however, glad she had called and not about to turn down her invitation to dinner. They agreed that B.J. would pick him up at his house around four.

Meanwhile, B.J. and her mother visited a travel agent who speedily and efficiently took care of Bertie's transportation to, and accommodation needs in Tucson, Arizona. At 11:00 p.m. the next day, Bertie would be winging her way south like a migratory bird in reverse. Her return date was left open until she knew how she liked it in the desert and determined how much her condition improved.

Over lunch afterward, B.J. was touched and amused by her mother's obvious excitement and anticipation at this imminent change of scene.

"My head is spinning," Bertie exclaimed. "So this is life in the fast lane."

"Yup." B.J. munched lettuce and inwardly blessed Floyd Morrison for making this possible. If their paths hadn't happened to cross at that trade show in Denver she wouldn't be in Spokane now, she wouldn't be in a position to help her mother now, *and* she would never have gotten to know Derek Coleman.

The possibility of the latter distressed her more than it should, given the fact that all they were destined to be was... friends.

B.J. sighed, and suddenly deflated, scraped back her chair. "Let's hit Nordie's, Mom, and see what stunning outfits we can find for you to take."

They shopped until Bertie, at least, very nearly dropped. "I'll never wear all this," she protested, but with a gleam in her eye and a smile on her lips. "I'm not a well woman...."

"*Here* you're not a well woman, Mother. *There* you'll be as good as new."

"I'll certainly look as good as new, won't I?"

"Clothes make the man, as they say. Or, in your case, the woman." B.J. held a gaily patterned camp shirt up against Bertie's chest, wrinkled her nose and put it back. "I want you to have fun, Mom. It's long overdue."

"You need more fun in your life, too, darling." Across racks of resort wear, Bertie tried to catch her daughter's eye. "And a man to love."

B.J. thought of Derek Coleman and evaded her mother's gaze. Her motions jerky, she riffled through a display of walking shorts. "I don't think that's in the cards for me, Mother."

"Then, perhaps it's time you changed your game."

"I'm not a gambler, Mom. And I don't play games."

"Everyone plays games to some extent, B.J. What is life, but a game of chance?"

"Humph." B.J.'s delicate snort was tinged with bitterness. "No wonder, then, that some of us have the cards stacked against us."

B.J. checked the address on the slip of paper twice, hoping she might have misread it, hoping this dismal neighborhood was not really where Justin was growing up. Unfortunately it was. She climbed up a sagging staircase to the second floor and knocked on the dirt-stained, peeling door marked *2B*.

A flaming redhead in a tight fluorescent skirt opened the door. Green eyes heavily outlined in black swept B.J.'s understated taupe slacks and matching suede jacket before settling on her face with wary hostility. "Yeah?"

"Oh. Hello. I—" B.J. momentarily forgot what she wanted to say. Was *this* Justin's mother? "Mrs. Andrews?"

"Ms."

"Oh. Of course. I'm B. J. Rawlings, a friend of Mr. Coleman. I—"

"Derek's friend, huh? He said you'd stop by." Once more the woman's assessing gaze swept her, but it was friendlier now. She stepped back and opened the door wider. "Come on in."

One glimpse at the apartment's interior was enough to convince B.J. she would rather not. "Thanks," she said, "but if Justin's ready...? You see, my mother's out in the car, waiting for us."

The woman's arched, penciled brow conveyed skepticism, but all she said was, "Sure. Jussy," she called into the room, "Derek's lady's here! So, Derek's out of town?" she remarked, turning back to B.J. while they waited for Justin to come.

"Yes. His father suffered a heart attack."

"Tough." The woman looked genuinely sympathetic. "You tell him I'm thinking of him when he calls, okay?"

"I will." B.J. found herself warming toward the redhead. There was something artless and endearing about her, in spite of the overdone makeup and slinky attire. She offered a tentative smile. "You have a very nice son, Ms. Andrews."

"He's okay." B.J.'s smile was returned. "And call me Starburst." When B.J.'s eyes widened at the name, she laughed. "Beats Marjorie, don't you think?"

"Is that your name? Marjorie?"

Starburst wrinkled her nose. "Awful, ain't it?"

"Beats Bertha Joanne," B.J. said dryly. "That's the name I got stuck with."

They laughed. "Jussy always looks forward to his weekends with Derek," Starburst said. "That's one nice guy you got there."

"Well, I don't really have him, you know. He and I—"

"Ready, Mom." Justin, his dark hair damp and slicked back from a recent combing, appeared in the doorway next to his mother.

"Hi." He shot B.J. an uncertain little smile, no doubt remembering her helter-skelter flight scene.

"Let me look at you." Starburst fussed with the denim jacket he wore over a T-shirt and jeans, all of them wrinkled but clean. "Now you behave for the lady, okay?" She kissed his cheek. "And when you get home, you go straight inside and keep the door locked till I get here."

"But where will you be?" B.J. asked, frowning. Surely the boy wouldn't be left on his own in this place? He was only ten. "Don't you have a sitter?"

Starburst's expression said, Yeah, sure. And a butler, too. "I work, " she said curtly. "But Jussy'll be fine. Won't you, hon?"

"Derek lets me stay at his house some Saturdays," Justin volunteered, a ring of hopeful suggestion in his tone.

"Yes, he does, doesn't he?" B.J. was thinking fast. The spare room was just sitting there. On the other hand, what did she know about entertaining little boys? But then, again, wasn't that erector set of hers down in the basement somewhere? "You could stay with me tonight, if you'd like...."

Justin beamed. "You mean it? Mom, can I?"

"If you're sure?" Starburst queried B.J.

B.J. had never been less sure of anything in her life. But just as she had in Derek's office, once again something made her wordlessly nod, Yes, when every instinct told her no would be the much wiser reply.

* * *

It was nearly nine o'clock and Justin was explaining the rudiments of poker to B.J. when the phone rang.

"I'll get it," B.J. called up to her mother, running out into the hall to where the downstairs phone sat next to the coatrack on a small drop-leaf table. "Hello?"

"Hello."

Even without the slightly husky emphasis on the second syllable, B.J. would have known that mellow baritone. Her pulse sped up.

She pressed a hand to her heart. "Derek. Hi. How's your father?"

"Improving, thank you. They moved him out of intensive care this morning."

"Thank God."

"Right." A small pause followed. B.J. could hear Derek breathing, which somehow made her own breath catch. "You knew it was me," he finally said, his tone warm and intimate. "Were you thinking of me, Bertha Joanne?"

Friends, B.J. reminded herself as her heart tripped along in overdrive. *We're just friends.*

She forced a little laugh. "It's hard not to, with your Little Brother in my living room, teaching me poker and prefacing everything with 'Derek says.'"

"Teaching you poker?"

"Yup. Red deuces and one-eyed jacks are wild."

"Oh, boy." Derek groaned. "Whatever you do, don't let him talk you into playing for money. That kid's a cardsharp."

"Funny, but I sensed that." B.J. felt much more at ease with this kind of banter. "The way he one-handedly shuffled the deck made me suspect he'd played a time or two."

"The little hustler regularly robs me blind." Derek chuckled, but there was no trace of laughter in his voice when he quietly added, "I owe you for this, B.J."

"Don't be silly." There she was, breathless again. "I love having him here. We thought we'd drop in on Baby tomorrow."

That announcement brought on another chuckle. "You invested in armor, did you?"

"Ha-ha!"

"I'm glad to hear his unintentional mauling didn't scare you away permanently. I would have hated to part with that dog."

What was Derek saying? That he would let the dog go, rather than part with her?

Don't be silly, B.J. told herself. He's joshing again. "Yeah, well, everyone deserves a second chance."

"I'm glad to hear you feel that way, Ms. Rawlings."

"And why is that, Mr. Coleman?"

"Because I'd like to have you back out to my house again. How about next weekend?"

"That's Easter."

"Exactly. We'll color Easter eggs with Justin."

"I wouldn't know how."

"Just one more thing for me to teach you, then."

Keep it light, girl. "Dare I ask what other things you think you can teach me?"

"I don't know, Bertha Joanne. Dare you?"

With her heart in her throat, B.J. couldn't speak for a moment. She told herself he was only teasing, but the husky tone of his voice told her otherwise. Taking a deep breath, this time she did say, "No, I don't think so."

"But you will," Derek assured her quietly. "Soon. I'm counting on it."

Chapter Nine

After waving Bertie off at Spokane International Airport, B.J. was glad of Justin's company. Up until today, *she* had always been the one doing the leaving. It seemed strange, and it was more painful than she would have thought, being the person left behind.

Driving along Geiger Boulevard on their way back to I-90, a departing jet roared overhead.

"There she goes," Justin cried, his nose pressed to the window. "Wow!"

Yeah, wow! B.J. silently echoed. She was feeling melancholy, reflecting that another chapter in her life was closing. There was no doubt in her mind that her mother would both need and want to spend increasingly longer periods in a desert climate from now on. Her health being what it was, Bertie really couldn't tolerate the Eastern Washington winters any longer, it made sense to take steps that would ensure she didn't have to.

Perhaps it was time to sell the house. B.J. recalled that as recently as last summer *she* had been the one against putting it on the market. At that time the idea of sorting through her father's things and throwing most of them away had still been as abhorrent as it had been just after he had died. Those things of his—his clothes, his tools, his books and the house were all she had left of him, she had stubbornly maintained. How could she let them go, toss them out? How could Bertie?

After that first awful year following her father's death, her mother had visibly shaken off the cloak of depression she had worn like widow's weeds. And though part of B.J. had been glad to have her mother happy again, another part had wondered at and resented Bertie's resiliency. Increasingly, the house, as well as John Rawlings's things, had become a bone of contention of sorts between mother and daughter.

But suddenly, now, B.J. realized it was time—past time—to let go of it all. Time to look forward, not back— time for both Bertie and herself to chart a new course.

She resolved to discuss the sale of the house with her mother the moment she called to say she had arrived in Tucson.

Just making the decision had B.J. feeling as if a ten-ton boulder had been rolled off her chest. With a quick grin at Justin, she burst into an impromptu and rusty rendition of "Old MacDonald Had a Farm," and by the second verse he had happily chimed in.

Singing at the top of their lungs, they exited the freeway at Division Street and made their way north past the garish parade of fast-food restaurants, shopping centers, gas stations and car dealerships that lined the bustling thoroughfare which doubled as State Route 395. The only stop they made on their way back to Derek's house was at a supermarket, where they bought the biggest beef bone they could find as a present for Baby.

The boarding kennel was only about a mile down the road from Derek's place. The man who owned it, Bill Munroe, bred and sold Great Danes and, in fact, Baby was the whelp of one of his prizewinning bitches. B.J. had phoned earlier to ask if it would be all right to visit, and so it took only moments before Baby bounded into the large fenced exercise yard where Justin and B.J. were waiting. Prepared for the dog's exuberant greeting, B.J. braced herself, but found she wouldn't have needed to.

At a sharp command from Justin, Baby came to a skidding halt in front of B.J. and sat. Tongue lolling, hindquarters wagging, he cocked his head and at another command from Justin politely offered his paw.

Somewhat gingerly B.J. took it in hand. The paw was warm, she realized with some surprise, and its pads felt slightly tough, like a work-roughened hand. The sleek fur on top was silky. With Justin's encouragement, she gave it a gentle shake. "Hello, Baby," she said brightly. "Remember me?"

Baby's head tilted the other way and the speed with which his tail swept the ground sent little sticks and pebbles flying.

"Good dog," Justin praised, adding in an aside to B.J., "See, he likes you," just as Baby sprang to his feet and in a reenactment of their first meeting launched himself at B.J. with panting glee.

Flat on her back in the dirt, B.J. was proud of the fact that this time she neither screamed nor fainted.

B.J. spent a large part of the following week doing business in Portland, Oregon. It wasn't until late Thursday night that she got back to Spokane. Tired and lonely in the empty house, she crept into bed, glad her days in the house would now be numbered. Bertie had been ecstatic at the prospect of sharing a nice new condominium with her daughter.

At nine the next morning, Good Friday, a real estate agent came to look at the house. By ten o'clock it was listed and by noon a lockbox hung by the porch door and a sign rose up from among the daffodils. After calling Bertie with the good news, B.J. went to the office to catch up on accumulated paperwork.

Shortly before leaving for home, Derek's secretary buzzed Cally, who in turn buzzed B.J. "Mr. Coleman on line three."

"Hello, Derek? Are you back?" B.J. couldn't keep a tone of unbusinesslike gladness out of her voice, and colored when Muriel Cooper, not Derek, came back with a brisk, "I'll just put you through, Ms. Rawlings."

Chagrined, B.J. replied with notable reserve to Derek's cheery, "Hi, there, gorgeous."

"Good afternoon."

"Brrr." Derek made his teeth chatter. "Do I sense a return of the Ice Age?"

"Sorry." Feeling silly now, B.J. relaxed in her chair. "A thaw just set in." Her voice warmed in tandem with her emotions. "Are you home?"

"If you mean in Spokane, no. But I will be sometime late tomorrow."

"Late, huh? Justin will be disappointed." Not only Justin, B.J. thought, her heart sinking. "We had hoped you'd be here in time for a picnic lunch."

"*We*, Bertha Joanne? You, too?"

The quietness of Derek's tone made B.J.'s blood quicken. Habit, as much as a quick resurgence of longtime insecurities, made her grope for a disclaimer. "Actually what I meant was—"

"Don't," Derek interrupted. "Please don't scramble to cover up honest emotions. We like each other. Haven't we agreed on that much, at least?"

Had they? B.J. curved her neck and shoulder around the phone, cradling it almost as if it were her lover. Mercy—how inadequate the word "like" was in describing the feelings which filled her heart to bursting. But then she thought sadly that Derek had no way of knowing that she loved him, just as there was no way she would ever be able to tell him.

And so, with the acceptance that her true feelings for Derek would forever stay locked in her heart, agreement with his choice of words came out as a tremulous sigh. "Y-yes."

"Well, then, what's wrong with looking forward to each other's company?"

B.J. closed her eyes. "Nothing, I s'pose."

"Ahh, Bertha Joanne." Derek's shuddering exhalation touched her like a caress, and she trembled as he added, "You're going to make me work for every inch of progress, aren't you?"

B.J.'s eyes fluttered open. She frowned. Progress? As in moving forward, as in moving toward a goal of some kind? "I don't know what you mean."

"Don't you? Don't you really?"

"No, I—"

"Then allow me to spell it out for you," Derek said. "Friendship is fine, it's a beginning. But I want more. I want *you*, Bertha Joanne. In my bed—in my life. So now you know."

Had it not been for Justin, B.J. would have gotten in her car and driven as far *away* from Derek Coleman and his incendiary pronouncements as possible. To Acapulco maybe, or better yet, Tombouctou! How dare he drop a bombshell like that and then hang up? She had sat there, frozen with shock and with the phone still clamped to her ear, until Cally had walked in and gently pried it out of her grip.

"Bad news?" Cally had asked.

To which, B.J. recalled, she had replied with a brilliant, "Huh?"

"That man is impossible," she groused to Justin as they walked out of the store with bags of groceries. It was ten o'clock Saturday morning and they were on their way out to Derek's. "Here it was his idea that we color Easter eggs, and now he won't even be here in time to do it. Have you ever colored eggs before, Justin?"

"Nuh-uh. Mom always got me a basket of candy eggs, though." He squinted up at B.J. "Did you get candy eggs when you were a kid?"

"No, I didn't."

"Did you color eggs?"

"Nope, didn't do that, either."

"How come?"

"Well, I guess my Pop didn't believe in that kind of stuff." B.J. shrugged. "He wasn't much for doing kids' things, you know?"

"How come?"

B.J. frowned. "I don't know." Though more and more lately she had condemned the way her father had brought her up, it had never occurred to her to question her father's motives.

"Maybe his dad didn't believe in kid stuff, either," Justin suggested.

B.J. stopped walking and looked down at the boy. "You know something, Jus? I bet that's exactly right. How'd you get so smart?"

Looking away, Justin flushed with abashed pleasure. "I dunno."

With both arms full, B.J. couldn't reach out and touch him as she would have liked, so she just playfully bumped a hip against his shoulder and said, "C'mon. We've got a picnic to get underway."

"And eggs to color?" Justin added with a hopeful lift in his voice.

"You betcha. How difficult can it be, right?"

The process, B.J. discovered, wasn't so much difficult as it was fraught with pitfalls and messes.

With a successful picnic behind them, a phone call to Mandy had gotten her the "recipe" for hard-boiled eggs.

"You have *got* to be the only woman on this entire planet who doesn't know how to boil an egg," Mandy had exclaimed with patent disgust. "I mean, really!"

"I happen to detest eggs and never eat the stinky things," B.J. had defended herself, "but I do *so* know how to boil them. Put water in pot, put pot on stove, put eggs in water. Any idiot knows that."

Mandy had wisely withheld comment.

"For how *long* they have to boil before they're hard is what I need to know," B.J. had added. "Derek has a cookbook, but it doesn't mention Easter eggs anywhere."

Mandy had muttered something unintelligible before asking, "Are you bringing the water to a boil first and then adding the eggs? Or are you putting them into the cold water and bringing both to a boil at the same time?"

"What on earth difference does it make?" B.J. had demanded, exasperated with Mandy who, in her opinion, was strutting her own culinary superiority in a most unbecoming fashion.

"Trust me, it makes a difference."

"All right." B.J. had done a mental coin toss. Heads, she put the eggs into the boiling water; tails, into cold. "Boiling."

"All right, then, five or six minutes ought to do it."

"But which is it exactly? Five or six?"

"Doesn't matter. Even if they cook a bit longer, they're all right."

B.J. took Mandy at her word. When the water came to a boil, she plopped in half a dozen eggs, and went off into the living room to help Justin with the jigsaw puzzle they had found on Derek's bookshelf. Soon they were both immersed.

"What's that smell?" Justin asked, sniffing, about half an hour later.

B.J. had absently sniffed once or twice before, wondering if perhaps Baby had been as discourteous as to... But this smell was different, not only sulfurous but acrid, too. Good grief, this was...

"The eggs!"

All three of them, B.J., Justin and Baby, leaped to their feet and practically tripped over each other in their haste to get to the kitchen. The dog got there first, took one look and one sniff and fled.

B.J. was tempted to do the same when she saw the mess she had created. Obviously leaving the burner control setting on "high" had been her first mistake. Not setting a timer, her second. Her third mistake, she concluded grimly, was letting Derek Coleman talk her into this stunt in the first place.

"Look at them." This from Justin, in a tone of awe. "Yuck."

Amen to that. The water had boiled away, the pot and the bottom-most four eggs were charred and smoking, and *all* of the eggs had exploded into abstract shapes.

Using a kitchen towel for a pot holder and wishing she had a free hand with which to hold her nose, B.J. gingerly and two-handedly picked the pot up by its scorching hot metal handle and carried it to the sink. For lack of anything better, she turned on the tap. Water hit the eggy mess with a hiss of steam and a renewed burst of noxious effluvium.

Justin, two fingers pinching his nostrils shut, had the belated presence of mind to turn on the exhaust fan over the stove. "I guess we won't get to color eggs now, huh?" he queried nasally and with visible disappointment.

The sight of him, so small and woebegone, wrenched B.J.'s heart. "What?" she exclaimed, "let one little mishap spoil the fun? Never!" She ruffled his hair. "Get another pot, Jus, and get ready for round two."

This time they stayed by the stove. "See," B.J. quipped, as the two of them stood watching the eggs rumble around in the boiling water, "it's not true that a watched pot doesn't boil."

She answered Justin's "oh brother" glance with an uncaring shrug, but inside she felt a glow the likes of which rivaled the glow Derek could make her feel. How easy it would be to love this little boy, and how easy to pretend he was hers. That this kitchen was hers, that this house was hers. And Derek's...

The timer went *ding* and they rushed the pot to the sink. Pushing the messy one aside, they ran cold water over the second batch.

"Now we'll let them cool for a bit," B.J. told Justin, "and then we'll get to the fun part." She glanced at the clock. It was going on five. "Why don't we get some dinner preparations under way. Let's see..." She opened the freezer compartment. "There's a chicken in here and some steaks. What'll it be?"

"Chicken. I *love* chicken."

"All right, then, turn the oven to— Wait, let me check the cookbook. Chicken, chicken... Chicken, roasted— here it is." B.J. scanned the brief instructions. "Oven to four-fifty to start, it says. Do that for me, Justin. Twenty to twenty-five minutes per pound. All right now, where's a pan?"

They found the broiling pan in the drawer underneath the oven. B.J. took the chicken out of its plastic wrapping, rinsed it under the faucet and dried it with paper towels. "Now this is still frozen," she said in an instructive tone to Justin, "so when you set the timer, add a half an hour."

Into the oven went the chicken. Rubbing her hands, feeling housewifely and competent, B.J. glanced at Justin, reading instructions. "What do we need for the coloring?"

"Some more boiling water."

"No problem." B.J. filled a teakettle and set it to boil. "What'll we eat besides chicken?"

"Macaroni and cheese. It's my favorite."

"Really?" B.J. arched a brow. "Is that good nutrition?"

"Yep, it is. Derek even said so."

"Well, if Derek even said so it must be true," B.J. agreed solemnly. "Let's see if he has any..."

He did, and after reading *those* instructions, B.J. got out another pot and set more water to boil. The teakettle whistled, they poured the water into several bowls, Justin plunked a dye tablet in each and after a few moments was ready to start on his eggs.

"Later we can draw pictures on them," he said to B.J., "but first I want to color these so that half of each egg is one color and half another. How can I do that, B.J.?"

"Hmm." She frowned thoughtfully. "Give me a minute to come up with something. First, though—" She opened the refrigerator and rummaged in the crisper. "We need a vegetable for our dinner."

She pulled out some slimy lettuce, grimaced and tossed it toward the sink. It landed with a splash in the ruined pot of eggs.

"There's nothing in here that's edible except carrots." She straightened. "I guess we'll have carrots."

"Yuck."

"Never mind. They're good for you." She washed them, cut them up in chunks and put them into the last remaining pot in Derek's cupboard. Covering them with water, she set them to boil, too.

"Now—" She turned to Justin. "About those eggs..." She pondered a moment, then snapped her fingers. "I got it. Some string. You look through those drawers, I'll look over here."

Justin found some. B.J. fashioned an adjustable loop at the end of it, looped it over an egg and pulled it taut. "Watch," she said, and carefully lowered the egg halfway into the dye. "See? And when you want to do the other end, you take these tongs here and carefully turn the egg over."

Baby barked. The door leading from the garage into the kitchen squeaked open. Justin swung around, the tongs caught the rim of the bowl, and contents sloshing, sent it skittering to the edge of the counter. B.J. caught it, and brick-egg dye trickled down the front of her white sweatshirt. Justin's egg slipped from the loop and dropped to the floor.

"What the hell...?" Derek stood thunderstruck, absently fending off the dog's affectionate greeting, his eyes widening at the scene before him. Billows of steam issued from several pots on the stove and boiling water hissed and sizzled on the burners. Something smelled like rotten eggs and charred remains... The sink was a disaster. Black smoke rose from the oven.

"We're doing Easter eggs."

"We're cooking dinner."

B.J. and Justin both spoke at once and both wore almost identical expressions of pride mingled with apprehension as they stared back at him. "I hope you're hungry," B.J. added.

Any sane person's appetite would have fled at the sights and smells before him, but, then, Derek didn't consider himself altogether sane where Bertha Joanne Rawlings was concerned.

"Starved," he said, and dropping his bags where he stood advanced on the well-meaning perpetrators. "Don't I get a hug hello?" he asked Justin, but turned a challenging eye on B.J. when the boy rushed to comply.

Derek kept his gaze locked on hers even as he bent to hug Justin back, and when they drew apart and the boy stepped away he opened his arms to her. "Come here," he commanded softly.

B.J.'s warring emotions were clearly visible in the depths of her sapphire eyes. And then, much like a swimmer about to execute a dive, she inhaled deeply and moved toward him.

Derek's arms enfolded her. B.J. stood stiffly for a moment. She trembled. Derek's embrace tightened, and with a ragged sigh she sagged against him. This was how it would be if she really did belong in this kitchen, in this house, she thought, and pain stabbed her heart. She pressed her cheek to his chest and hugged his waist. "Oh, Derek."

Derek's heart expanded. For a moment he rested his chin on the crown of her hair, savoring the closeness, the feel of her warm, pliant body against his. When had she become so dear to him? he marveled, and immediately answered himself with a rueful, inner smile. That night he had seen her on top of that ladder trying to steam off the wallpaper. And again, right here in his home, recuperating from Baby's overwhelming welcome.

He had let her glimpse his feelings then, and—clearly frightened—she had run. Tonight, he vowed, he wouldn't let her. Tonight, they would confront what was happening between them and come to terms with it.

Gently he nudged her head until she lifted it from his chest and raised her face to his. "I'm going to kiss you," he said and, before she could protest, did. Thoroughly.

"Hey, you guy-uy-s," Justin singsonged, "something's bur-ning."

I know, Derek thought, me. He felt B.J. struggle, try to speak, and clasped her more tightly. Not yet. Not yet. But the spell was broken, and besides he smelled the smoke now, too. The same as when he came in, only worse.

He relaxed his hold and B.J. spun away. "The chicken," she panted, pressing a hand to her chest even as she rushed to the stove. She tore open the oven door and stepped back as a blast of smoke choked her. It stung her eyes, drawing tears. "Oh, noooo..."

From the sidelines, Justin observed, "It's ruined, isn't it, huh?"

Derek shot him a glance of warning, waving his hands to clear some of the smoke. One look at the crisply charcoal-breasted fowl told him it was beyond help. Slamming the oven door shut, he turned every knob on the stove to the Off position, folded his arms across his chest and leveled a look of inquiry at B.J.

"What," he smiled mildly, "did you think you were doing?"

B.J. slanted him a fulminating sideways glare. "I was *cooking*."

She enunciated the word with such venom, Derek almost flinched. He raised his brow. "You don't like to cook?"

"I *loathe* it."

"Tried it much, have you?"

"Twice."

Watching thunderclouds darken B.J.'s sky-blue eyes and flags of temper brighten her cheeks until they matched the red stain on her shirt, Derek felt an almost overpowering urge to laugh. However, some sense of self-preservation told him it wouldn't be wise to give in to it. He had to bite the inside of his cheek, though, before he could ask, "What was it you cooked the first time?"

"Scrambled eggs." She shuddered. "In peanut butter."

He did lose it then. Grabbing her shoulders, he dropped a hard kiss on her pouting lips, then crushed her in his arms and laughed aloud.

B.J. stood ramrod-straight and unyielding. "How was I to know you can't cook with the stuff? It's called butter, isn't it?"

Derek laughed harder.

"Dammit, it's not funny." B.J. had never been so mortified, nor felt so inadequate. How dare he laugh? Something touched her hand and she jerked it away.

"B.J., are... are you mad?" Justin asked in a small voice.

B.J. glanced down into his worried face, caught sight of the wobbling lower lip and gave a cry of dismay. "No."

Derek, too, had heard the boy. Abruptly, amusement was replaced by concern. Together, he and B.J. dropped to their knees in front of their young friend.

"Oh, Justin," B.J. crooned, taking him into her arms. "I'm not mad, darling. Not really. And certainly not at you."

"A-at D-Derek, then?"

"No, no. Not at Derek, either." Over the boy's head, she sent Derek a look of chagrin, then set Justin away a bit so she could look him in the face. "I guess I'm mad at myself—" with a rueful smile, she smoothed his hair "—because I made such a mess of things. I even ruined boiled eggs, for crying out loud."

"That wasn't your fault."

"Oh, yeah? Whose fault was it, then—Baby's? Huh?"

That made him giggle.

Derek stood back on his heels and took it all in. Was this the woman who claimed to be inept with children? She had Justin all but doing cartwheels for her.

Somewhere in the course of his vigil by his father's bedside, Derek had admitted to himself that what he felt stirring within for B.J. was the real thing, and that what he wanted with her were the things that his mother and father had shared for more than thirty-eight years: mutual respect, a lifetime of devotion and caring. But he had to let go of his fears first and learn how to open his heart again.

He had almost been ready to offer B.J. everything, and the sight of her now affirmed those feelings.

So what if she couldn't cook and even hated the chore, just as Margo had? So what if she detested housework, again as Margo had? So what if her strengths lay in areas that by some were still considered strictly male domains? None of those things made her Margo's clone, as he had cynically assumed in the early stages of their acquaintance.

He had learned long since that B.J. was warm and incredibly giving—witness her caring relationship with her mother, with Mandy Jenks's family, with Justin...

And, Derek told himself almost grimly, she cared for him, too. Why else would she be here doing—he cast a wry look around the disaster area that was his kitchen—all this?

B.J. cared, all right. Perhaps she even loved him. All he had to do was make her admit it. And he would.

Tonight.

Chapter Ten

Teamwork got the kitchen back in shape, teamwork transformed ordinary hard-boiled eggs into artistic masterpieces and teamwork made short shrift of the giant super-combo pizza Derek ordered in.

Their tummies full, B.J., Justin and Derek trooped into the living room, picked at the puzzle for a bit and then decided to curl up on the couch and watch a video. While Justin and B.J. went through Derek's tape library, Derek brought a couple of armloads of wood in from outside and lit a fire in the fireplace.

Wiping his hands on the seat of his jeans, he came up behind them. "Finding anything?"

B.J.'s eyes danced as she glanced back at him across one shoulder. She was clearly getting a kick out of Justin's solemn-faced contemplation of the two tapes in his hands.

"We're having a problem deciding between *Lethal Weapon II* and *Crocodile Dundee*."

"Do I get a vote?"

"No," Justin and B.J. replied simultaneously, and Justin added, "Okay, this one," after another moment of indecision. He handed *Lethal* to Derek and put the other tape back.

"That's the one I would've picked," Derek groused with a companionable wink at B.J.

Charmed by Derek's easy and affectionate manner, and inwardly marveling at how different he was—or had become—from the hardened cynic who had regarded her as something of an opportunistic Jezebel, B.J. settled herself into one corner of the soft leather couch. The fantasy she had been half subconsciously living all day, the one that had her in the role of Derek's wife and Justin's mother, was still with her. She felt at ease and very much...content. Tucking her feet up under her, she once again banished the tiny voice that whispered, It can never be, kiddo.

"Since I haven't seen either one of those films," she declared, "I'm easy."

"Hmm..." Derek wiggled his brows, holding an imaginary cigar between thumb and forefinger, Groucho-style. "I'll keep that in mind, m'dear."

Predictably, B.J. blushed. Delighted by her reaction, Derek chuckled as he got the VCR ready to roll. His good humor increased even more when he noticed that Justin had curled up in the sofa's other corner, leaving the middle for him.

He plunked himself about an inch or so away from B.J. and slanted her an innocent glance. "Not crowding you, am I?"

His lingering glance called forth a decidedly warm response. B.J. had to bite her lip to keep a giddy smile off her face, as she answered his facetious inquiry with a look that was meant to convey she was on to his tactics.

Derek's grin was unrepentant. Lazily turning his head, he winked at Justin who was munching peanuts and every now and then feeding a couple to Baby who, even sitting on the floor as he was, was eye-level with the boy. Justin was also in charge of the remote controls.

"Let 'er roll, sport," Derek told him with an affectionate slap on his flannel pajama-clad knees. Being ready for bed had been one of Derek's prerequisites to the boy's staying up and watching the film. "He rarely lasts the distance," he had confided to B.J. in an undertone. "This way I can just scoop him up and put him to bed without waking him."

As Justin fast forwarded through some previews and the film's credits, Derek stretched, yawned and then just naturally let his right arm settle behind B.J.'s head on the sofa's backrest.

B.J., her heart increasingly on fast forward with Derek so close, pretended not to notice, just as she pretended not to be disturbed by the solid length of his thigh touching her tucked-up knees. Soon she was so engrossed in the film's breakneck action, as well as amused by the fast-paced repartee, that she was able to forget to worry about Derek's unsettling proximity for entire minutes. Even when he casually shifted closer and moved his arm from the backrest to her shoulders, her attention remained on the movie.

So involved was she, that in response to Derek's slight nudge, she absently bent forward to allow his arm to slip around her more comfortably and completely. With a blissful sigh, she scooted down a bit on the seat and let her head relax against his shoulder.

Justin, too, came looking for a cuddle. Reversing his previous back-into-corner sitting position, he now propped himself against Derek's free side, and after some minutes of that, slid down, rolled onto his side and rested his cheek on Derek's thigh.

As B.J. and Derek softly chuckled at a comical scene, long, even breaths audibly announced Justin's arrival in dreamland.

After signaling B.J. to silence, Derek carefully got up off the couch and carried the sleeping child from the room.

B.J. muted the video's sound and, intrigued, followed Derek into a room in which there were two twin beds divided by a common nightstand. On it stood a lamp, the base of which was in the shape of a football, and a framed snapshot of Justin and his mother. On the wall opposite was a dresser with a collection of books stacked on top. Some framed Norman Rockwell prints adorned the walls and a baseball bat and glove lay by the straight chair at the foot of Justin's bed. His backpack and discarded clothes were in a heap on the spare bed.

B.J. hurried to fold back the blue-and-white striped bedspread and the sheet and blanket beneath. Derek's arm brushed hers as he bent and lowered Justin onto the mattress. Their bodies brushed, too, as B.J. gently tucked the covers around the boy.

How sweet, how innocent a child looks in sleep, she marveled, noting the sweep of luxurious lashes on a flushed, downy cheek and the bow of a mouth which, when Justin was awake, was never allowed to look so vulnerable. Giving in to a sudden need, she softly kissed Justin's smooth forehead.

As her lips rested for one brief instant against the boy's downy skin, a desperate sense of loss engulfed her. The pain, the niggling voice, all of her demons were now in control. Never, they told her, never would she have the pleasure of watching a child of her own like this; never would she be able to have picnics or color Easter eggs or snuggle by the fire with a son or daughter who was hers. Never. Never...

Abruptly she straightened, bumping Derek. He stepped aside automatically, then watched, puzzled, as B.J. rushed from the room. More sedately, he followed and found her standing in the middle of the living room, arms tightly wrapped around her midsection, shoulders hunched. Her facial expression bleak, she was staring at the images flickering across the television screen, but Derek doubted she was consciously taking anything in.

He went to stand in front of her and with his forefinger lifted her chin so that she looked up at him. The despair in her eyes brought him a surge of pain.

"B.J.," he said, his voice tender-rough with concern. "Sweetheart, what is it?"

Her chin wobbled against his finger. He removed it, cupping instead the curve of her cheek as she bit her lip to still the tremor. She blinked against the sting of tears and with a broken, "Oh, Derek," let her forehead drop down to his shoulder.

"Tell me," Derek coaxed gently, closing his arms around her shivering form and drawing her close. "Don't shut me out, love. Tell me what's wrong."

She rolled her head back and forth in a negative motion, still hugging herself within his embrace. "I c-can't." Another shiver shook her, and with a plaintive, "Oh, Lord, I'm so cold," she huddled against him. "Warm me, Derek. Oh, please, please warm me."

"I will." All the love Derek had kept bottled up inside him burst from him now in an avalanche of tenderness. "Put your arms around me, sweetheart," he whispered hoarsely, and when she had complied, he pulled her body flush against his as if to absorb her into himself and infuse her with some of his heat. They stood as close as it was possible for two people to stand without being joined, and Derek gently rocked B.J. in his arms while his hands rubbed the length of her back with long, soothing and undemanding strokes.

Pressed against Derek's solid warmth, surrounded by his strength and his caring, B.J. felt cherished and loved in a way she never had before. The icy clump of hopelessness and despair that had chilled her to the marrow as she stood by Justin's bed began to melt. Her blood, which for a while seemed to have frozen, was being warmed now by Derek's closeness, by the rhythmic massage of his hands on her back. She felt like someone who had been adrift for too long, but who had finally found a safe harbor.

She couldn't have said precisely when it was she stopped feeling cherished and began feeling desired. And desir*ous*.

Perhaps it was when the steady beat of Derek's heart against hers became erratic, accelerated. Or maybe when the stroke of his hands lengthened, when they traced the curve of her spine, the swell of her buttocks and finally began to linger. Or maybe it was when one hand slid up her side, searched out her breast and took possession, or when the gentle rocking of their bodies from side to side became an arousing and mutual undulation of hips.

Derek groaned, his lips sought hers and, with a mewling cry of need B.J. opened for him. Their kiss was like a feeding frenzy of two starved souls. Their bodies straining, their hands were frantic in their search for naked skin, their mouths ravished and their tongues mated.

With one hand tunneling beneath Derek's shirt, B.J. reveled in the sleek ripple of muscle there, while her other hand boldly cupped a tight male buttock and urged his hardness more closely against her straining loins.

B.J.'s uninhibited response, her obvious arousal and undisguised need for him, ignited Derek's passions as no other woman ever had. Desire was at once tempered and fueled by the love he felt for her. His body's urgent demand to fully possess this woman was doubled and redoubled by an equally urgent need to cherish and protect.

Her hands were in his hair now, gripping, tugging and then on his shoulders holding on. Their mouths were avid in mutual exploration, their breaths a panting exchange of air. Spreading his legs, Derek gripped B.J.s bottom and lifted her until she was perfectly aligned for the ultimate act. He held her there for a quivering moment and then he carried her to his bedroom.

B.J., drunk on passion and desperate to show Derek the love she dared not put into words, made no conscious decision to share this night with him. She didn't have to. Everything that had transpired since Derek's homecoming had led her to this moment when he was laying her on his bed as carefully as if she were made of priceless Dresden porcelain. She welcomed his weight as he followed her down and kissed him back with a hunger and demand that matched his. She rolled with him onto her side, arched to accommodate his searching hand, and when he had released the clasp of her bra, her sigh of pleasure and anticipation shuddered into his mouth.

First his fingers, then his lips teased and tantalized, and the wondrous reality of his caresses far exceeded B.J.'s fevered expectations. Joy, fierce and exalting, brought tears to her eyes, and with a choked sob she clutched Derek's head and pressed him to her.

"I love you," she cried brokenly. "I love you, love you, lo—"

Derek's fiery possession of her lips cut short her litany of love. Hot and open, his mouth feasted on hers. Once again his tongue invited hers to join with his in a dance as old as time. And then he lifted his head. Eyes alight with love and burning with desire, he looked at her.

"I love you as I've never loved before," he said. His voice was rough and low and shaking with the force of his emotions. "I want you, Bertha Joanne." He kissed her eyes. "I need you, Bertha Joanne." He kissed her nose, her ears, the curve of her chin.

And all the while his hands roamed and stroked and teased and explored, until B.J. felt as if she would surely melt right into the mattress.

"I want to make you mine, Bertha Joanne Rawlings—I want to never let you go."

He kissed the corners of her mouth while his hand possessively came to rest low on the concavity of her stomach. His voice dropped to a gravelly, fervent whisper. "I want to marry you, Bertha Joanne, and I want to make a child with you..." his hand moved lower and urged her thighs apart "...starting right now."

"Oh, my God!" The wail of despair rose from deep within B.J.'s heart and ripped it to shreds. "What have I done?"

She had no right to be here, had no right to let Derek think she could be what he wanted, needed, her to be. With desperate strength she struggled out of Derek's embrace and scrambled off the bed.

Shocked into immobility, Derek lay on his side. Whirling, B.J. stared at him with eyes that were wild and unfocused. "I can't, don't you see?" she cried, her voice brittle as spun glass and already breaking. "I can't, I can't...."

Before Derek could gather his shattered wits enough to react, she had fled from the room. Seconds later, he was on his feet and running. His hand was on the knob of the front door when the engine of B.J.'s car roared to life. He was out the door and in his driveway just as, tires screeching, she reversed out of it.

Shoulders slumped, arms dangling at his sides, Derek helplessly watched the woman he loved speed away from him as if the very demons of hell pursued her.

Shortly after he arrived at the office on Monday morning, Derek found out what he hadn't been able to ascertain during a Sunday of intermittent calls to B.J.'s house. She had gone out of town.

Cally had a note for him. Turning the envelope over in his hands, curiously reluctant to open it, he found the back held no more clues to the contents than did the envelope's front on which was written a simple and impersonal "Derek Coleman."

He wondered if, after the passion they had shared little more than twenty-four hours before, her message would be equally impersonal. Would it say, *I made a mistake, I don't really love you?* Or would it say, *I hurt as much as you do?*

Grimly compressing his lips, Derek figured there was only one way to find out. His hand trembled slightly as he tore open the envelope. With his heart beating heavily in his chest, his eyes scanned the small sheet of paper.

Dear Derek—
I'm taking a few weeks to travel my territory. I apologize for Saturday night. For the way I departed, but especially for allowing things to get where such a departure became necessary. I've lied to you, if only by

omission, but believe me, you wouldn't love me and you never would have said those beautiful words to me if you'd known the truth. I'll treasure the memories, but when next we meet I'll pretend nothing ever happened between us. I trust you will, too.

B.J.

P.S. I've requested relocation to our Portland office.

Derek read the letter twice, then tore it into shreds, which he dropped into the wastebasket. Leaning back in his chair, he let his chin drop to his chest. Blindly, he stared at the hand he folded across his stomach. He was deep in thought.

I've lied to you.

He repeated the phrase in his mind, over and over, but he waited in vain for the reaction of outrage and betrayal a similar admission from Margo had elicited once upon a time. Sitting still and sightless in his chair, he searched his soul for what he did feel. Pain was uppermost, but not the pain of betrayal, nor the pain of having loved and lost.

His love for B.J. was unchanged. And it would take a whole lot more than a few scribbled sentences on a page of foolscap before he considered her lost.

No, the pain he felt was the pain of regret, of failure. *His* failure. He had been able to make her love him—and she did love him, he knew that as surely as he knew he loved her—yet he had failed to make her trust him.

What? Why? And how? Those words, those questions, nagged at him and demanded answers. What could be so terrible in her perception that she felt he wouldn't love her, wouldn't want her, if he knew? Why was she so afraid of taking that final step, of committing herself to him? Why was she so afraid of the commitment he had made to her? How could he help her, how could he make her see that, no matter what, he wanted her for now and always?

Slapping his hands on his knees, Derek resolutely got to his feet. He might not know the answers to those questions, he conceded grimly, but one thing he did know—he sure as hell wasn't going to sit around twiddling his thumbs and waiting for Bertha Joanne Rawlings to come to her senses while his—and her—future happiness hung in the balance.

B.J. had operated on automatic pilot from the moment she ran from Derek's house and sped down the road toward hers. Though she didn't consciously think it, she knew instinctively that if she stopped and considered *his* words and *her* pain, she would go stark, raving mad.

She had come to love Derek in ways she hadn't known it was possible to love. He kindled her passions, he stimulated her intellect, he challenged her ambitions. He evoked in her feelings of protective tenderness the likes of which she would never have thought herself capable of, even as he in turn made her feel cherished and safe.

It was magic.

But magic was illusion, wasn't it? Fantasy. A dream.

She had allowed herself to dream—for a little while. She had asked herself, What harm could it do? Love was something everyone craved, everyone needed, and she was no exception.

Derek loved her. She could see it in his eyes every time he looked at her, and she felt it every time he did as little as brush against her in passing. Awareness would sizzle between them at those times and communicate itself by the merest pause in whatever it was they were doing.

Oh, yes, long before he had said the words, she had known Derek loved her.

But if there was one thing B.J. had learned from her father, it was that love didn't come for nothing. It had to be earned. One had to be worthy.

For a few hours there at Derek's house she had allowed herself the illusion that she was worthy, and in so doing she had hurt not only herself, but Derek as well.

It was knowing the latter which had sent her running and had kept her in flight. Until tonight.

Tonight—Thursday evening, huddled in a hotel room in the town of Roseburg, Oregon—guilt, remorse, love, despair and an abiding sense of irreparable loss caught up with her and demanded recognition.

Pushing aside the barely tasted fast-food dinner she had brought to the room, B.J. pressed the heels of her hands into her eyes and willed away the weak and useless tears that threatened. She inhaled deeply, harshly. She would not cry.

She cried—and at the sharp rap at her door, jerked upright with a guilty start.

Furiously brushing at the unwanted tears, unable to stop them from falling, B.J. held her breath. Perhaps whoever it was would go away if they thought she wasn't there.

A key scratched in the lock. B.J.'s hand flew to her mouth and she watched with horror as the handle turned. The door opened.

Derek Coleman stepped into the room.

Chapter Eleven

Derek.

B.J.'s mind shaped the word, but no sound passed her lips, still shielded by the hand she held pressed to them. Eyes wide, the flow of her tears stemmed by shock, she watched as Derek calmly closed the door.

Her hand dropped to her lap and clutched the napkin still spread there from her uneaten dinner. Questions crowded her mind. She had left strict instructions with Cally to the effect of, Don't call me, I'll call you. So how had Derek known where to find her? How had he gotten here?

She tried to articulate her jumbled thoughts. "W-what...? H-how...?"

"Funny." Derek strode to the desk, switched on the lamp and dispelled the gloomy twilight in which B.J. and her misery had been content to huddle. "Those very words kept popping into my mind every time I thought of the way you ran from me. Again. I'm here to get some answers."

He pulled the straight chair away from the desk and straddled it. "Why are *you* here, Bertha Joanne?"

From the moment he opened the door, B.J. had been struggling mightily to gain control over her precarious emotions. Now, Derek's cool and aloof demeanor was exactly what she needed to buck her up.

She clasped her hands tightly in her lap. "I'm sure you're aware that Roseburg is a logging town, as well as part of my territory. I'm here on business, what else?"

Derek's nod was noncommittal. "Rough day?"

"What makes you think it was?"

He looked at her hands. "Call it a hunch." His expression was wry. "In addition to that white-knuckled finger-twisting going on in your lap."

B.J. felt, again, the pressure of tears and despised herself for the weakness. She knew that men had no patience with weak women, had no tolerance for women who reacted to every confrontation, every crisis, with tears. And Lord knew, she had already more than exhausted Derek Coleman's patience and tolerance with the melodramatic stunts she had pulled. She would not disgrace herself further by falling apart all over again.

"I got word today that we lost the Wanger order," she said, her voice hoarse with the strain of keeping it from breaking. "I...we...w-worked so h-hard—"

She ran out of words, as aware as she knew Derek had to be, that losing the Wanger order wouldn't have her cracking like this. It was the memories. Looking down at her hands, she remembered the meeting with the Wanger people they had had to postpone because of the blizzard. And then being stuck in the ditch in Derek's car, sharing body heat.... Kissing....

Raising her eyes to Derek's was a mistake. B.J. knew it the instant her gaze connected with his, and she read in their golden green depths the exact same memory of that snowbound kiss. She wanted to look away. She wanted, for the third time, to run. She couldn't do either.

The time for evasions, the time for running was past.

"Do you love me, Bertha Joanne?" Derek asked, his eyes drilling into hers, drilling into her heart.

B.J. swallowed. "Y-yes." And then, seeing a flash of pain so naked, so stark it made her own pain redouble, she reached out to him and cried, "Oh, Derek, how could I not? You've been...wonderful. You've been so much *more* than I've ever dreamed a man could be...."

In a flash, Derek was off the chair and on his knees in front of her. His hands gripped hers in a painful grip from which B.J. was nevertheless unwilling to free herself. "Then why?" he asked hoarsely. "Why?"

The moment of truth had come.

With her hands in Derek's and her heart already in his keeping, B.J. bowed to the inevitable. She would tell Derek the truth about herself and then the shoe would be on the other foot. The *running* shoe, that was. He would run as fast as she had, maybe faster.

"It's me, don't you see?" she said. Tears no longer threatened. The time for crying, too, had passed. A deep calm now pervaded her. "I'm not the woman you think I am."

B.J.'s serenity communicated itself to Derek. He, too, drew in a hard, steadying breath. "And what exactly kind of woman do you think I take you to be?" he asked.

B.J. blew out a rueful snuff of air. "Hard-nosed. Competitive. Successful."

Derek squeezed her hands. "You'll get no argument from me so far."

Her voice lowered, the words dragged. "Competent..."

"You bet."

"...smart..."

"In spades."

B.J.'s tone grew quieter yet. "...fertile and worthy—"

"Whoa." Derek's hands once again tightened around hers. He tugged, pulling her toward him until their faces were only inches apart. "Say that again, please."

"Worthy." Her breath, as she whispered the word, caressed his lips. Derek promised himself that soon he would kiss her.

"We'll deal with that one," he said, "after I've heard the one before that."

B.J. stared at his adamant expression and felt her heart break. "I said," she reiterated with painful clarity, "fertile."

Derek heard, but didn't immediately comprehend. His eyes searched hers as if for clarification for long, breathless moments during which every sound—the hum of cars on the freeway, the slam of doors in the hall, the dripping tap in the bathroom and the heavy beat of their hearts—became magnified a thousandfold.

"Oh, God," he groaned when the import of the word finally and irrevocably sank in. "Oh, God." With trembling hands he drew B.J. down onto the floor in front of him and hugged her tight.

At length he set her away just enough to look into her eyes again. They were dry. And as brilliantly bright as skies of blue on a cloudless summer day.

They were too bright, Derek realized. They were pain-bright. Tear-bright. And he felt a corresponding prick at the back of his own eyes.

"I'm sorry," he whispered hoarsely, resting his forehead against hers. "Oh, sweetheart, I'm so—"

"Don't you dare say it again." Mortified at being an object of sympathy, B.J. struggled out of Derek's embrace and onto her feet. "Never, *never* say that again. I can't have children, but I can have dignity. I'll hate you if you dare pity me."

"Pity you? Good Lord, woman—" Derek, too, surged to his feet. His hands balled into fists to keep from taking her by the shoulders and shaking her till her teeth rattled. "Times like this I'd dearly love to *strangle* you! Could you just once in the course of our discussions not ascribe to me *your* assumptions and interpretations of *my* motives and feelings? We wouldn't be in this sorry fleabag of a motel hundreds of miles from home if you'd had the guts to face issues head-on instead of running away from them."

"Oh, yeah?" Knowing Derek was right didn't matter. What mattered in the state of panic that always gripped B.J. when confronted on a personal level, was to pretend she didn't care. That's how she had coped in the painful years of grade and high school when the girls with whom she had longed to be friends had given her the cold shoulder. And that was how she had been able to bear it when Mark had charged her with being as sexless and cold as a fish....

"So who asked you to follow me to this so-called sorry fleabag?" she spluttered. "I didn't, that's for sure."

"You didn't because that would have been the honest thing to do," Derek charged.

"I didn't because I wanted to spare us both..." she flung up her hands "...this! This *shouting match!*"

"Better a shouting match than the silent treatment. Better to stand and fight than to run like a rabbit, Bertha Joanne."

"Don't call me that! Haven't I told you not to call me that?"

"It's your name, dammit! Like it or not, own up to it. Like it or not, own up to who you *are*. Own up to what you are—quit running from it. Quit beating your head against the wall, quit trying to be what you can't be. Where is it written that you have to be perfect, huh? Nobody's perfect, B.J., but most of us are able to come to terms with that. Most of us are content to do the best we can with what we have."

Somewhere in the course of Derek's impassioned harangue he had taken hold of B.J.'s shoulders and shaken them for emphasis. Now he released them so abruptly B.J. tottered back a few steps.

They stared at each other, each of them breathing hard.

"I can't help you deal with your ghosts, Bertha Joanne," Derek said quietly. His ire expended, he was weary now in the face of B.J.'s white-faced silence. "I can't help you at all, unless you stick around and talk to me."

He waited for her to say something, but B.J. continued to stand in frozen silence. Her hands were clasped, as if in prayer, and pressed to her mouth. Her eyes wide and unblinking, she turned toward the darkened window.

Derek's shoulders slumped. With a sigh, he headed for the door.

"Pop never wanted me the way I was," B.J. said hollowly from behind him. "All he wanted was a son."

With his hand on the doorknob, his heart pounding, Derek stayed to listen. But he didn't turn around.

"And so I did everything I could not to disappoint him. I dressed like a boy, acted like a boy, did with him all the things a boy does with his father. We hiked, we camped, we fished, we climbed. Some of the things I liked, some I hated, but I did them all because if I didn't, if I complained..."

B.J. stopped to take a shuddering breath. Derek let go of the doorknob. Slowly he turned. She had moved to the window and stood with one hand resting on the wall next to it. But she wasn't looking out. Her head was bowed.

"He had a way with words, Pop did," she said. "He could cut me to ribbons, make me feel less than worthless with just a few sentences. 'I have neither patience nor time for a spineless, sniveling female, *Bertha Joanne*,'" B.J. mimicked bitterly. "'If you want to be just another dumb blonde, that's fine with me, *Bertha Joanne*...'"

B.J. rubbed at her forehead, as if to erase the hurtful memories. Unable to banish them, her hand dropped to her side in a gesture of defeat. "He only called me by name when I angered him, and then he made it sound like an insult. I hated it. I hated the name and myself. I even hated my mother for a while, because I blamed her for my gender. With my father's encouragement, I resisted her every attempt to make me proud of my femininity. When I chopped off all my hair one time so I'd look more like a boy, Mom cried. Pop laughed and took me to his barber for a real boy's cut. Mom must have objected for once, because he never took me there again. But until well into high school I wore my hair very short.

"I had no friends. In grade school, the boys I wanted to play with didn't want me because I was a girl. The girls made fun of me, because of the way I dressed and acted. Later, in high school, when nature added insult to injury by making me sprout breasts and hips, the situation reversed somewhat. All sorts of boys wanted to spend time with me, and I was the one who rebuffed them. As for the girls...."

Shrugging, B.J. turned her back to the window and for the first time since she started her monologue was able to smile. "With the exception of Mandy, I considered them all beneath contempt...officially." Her smile faded. "Secretly, since by then I knew I'd never become the *son* my father wanted, I envied them. They knew who and what they were, they *flaunted* their gender, reveled in it. I, on the other, was neither fish nor fowl. I was B.J., and outward developments notwithstanding, on the inside I was as genderless as those two initials."

B.J. moved to the desk, trailed a finger across the imitation leather-bound services directory and slanted Derek a glance that was part self-deprecation, part apology. "I'll bet when you suggested we talk, this self-indulgent diatribe was not what you had in mind."

"Don't." Derek had stayed by the door all this time. Now he came back into the room. "What I had in mind was to get you to stop running long enough to examine what drives you. You're doing that." He touched her cheek, a gentle caress. "I'm sorry it hurts."

B.J. closed her eyes and relaxed into the caress. It felt so good, like a balm on the wounds of her spirit.

"I'm only sorry for the hurt I've caused you," she whispered, covering his hand with hers and letting it stay there a moment before she used it to draw his away from her face. She continued to clasp his hand, however, and stared down at it as she added, "I wish you didn't love me, Derek."

"But I do love you, Bertha Joanne. And your wish won't change that."

"There are so many women out there who are so much more worthy."

"Aha! I wondered when we'd get around to that." Derek pulled his hand out of hers and folded his arms across his chest. He leveled an expectant gaze at her. "Tell me about your unworthiness."

"Now you're laughing at me."

"Actually, I'm trying very hard not to. Why don't you explain to me why you think I should take your position seriously."

Pinned in place by Derek's arch regard like a note to a bulletin board, B.J. cast around helplessly for some pertinent evidence to support her claim that she was lacking. Unable to come up with anything better, she finally blurted, "Did you know that my father had to almost physically *drag* me from Camp Muir up to the summit of Mount Rainier? That it was only *his* determination, not mine, that got me up there? I was a coward; I was crying and throwing up...."

"Altitude sickness," Derek interjected calmly. "It happens. As you know *I* get carsick unless I'm the one doing the driving. Once I threw up all over my date and her father, who also happened to be my homeroom teacher. Neither one of them ever spoke to me again."

"Pop didn't speak to me for weeks after that climb, but he never told anyone else of my shame, either. I was grateful to him for that."

Derek clenched his jaw, forbidding himself the pleasure of voicing his thoughts on B.J.'s father.

"At the end of that summer we climbed Mount Si," B.J. said.

"And?"

"Same story."

"Great." Derek grimaced. "Me and my big mouth, telling Jack Carruthers you're a candidate for his Mountaineers."

"That's okay. I joined."

Derek's jaw dropped. "For heaven's sake, why?"

B.J. shifted uncomfortably. "It doesn't do to give into one's weaknesses."

"Another of Pop's homilies, is it?" This time Derek didn't bother to hide his contempt.

"In this instance, I happen to think he's right."

"Meaning there are other instances about which you've come to understand he wasn't right?"

B.J. picked up a cold French fry and eyed it with distaste. "Yes."

"Such as?"

"Such as he should've let me choose my own college major." She dropped the bit of potato as if it were something disgusting and raised her eyes to Derek's. "I wanted to become an English teacher, maybe a writer."

"I might not have met you then." Derek came to take her hands. "I would've been desolate."

B.J.'s smile was melancholy. "You would've found someone infinitely better suited—"

"Shh...." Derek's finger across B.J.'s lips silenced her. His eyes on hers were somber. "B.J., Bertha Joanne, listen to me because I'm only going to say this once. I love you. You. Warts and all. Will you marry me?"

Tears filled B.J.'s eyes. As soon as Derek lifted his finger, she whispered, "But don't you see, I can't? You want a family..."

"I want *you*. The rest will work itself out."

"You don't understand. More than one doctor has told me—"

"No." Derek gripped her upper arms, gave her a hard shake. "It's you who doesn't understand. You're afraid to make a commitment, you're afraid to be loved because you've allowed your father to convince you that you aren't *worthy* of love—Lord, but I detest that word," Derek ground out in an angry aside, "unless you're perfect. Aside from the fact that nobody's perfect, it's *his* standard of perfection that's messed you all up. There's no way you could ever have lived up to his expectations, don't you understand? Because they weren't grounded in reality. Don't you see that?"

"I do see it," B.J. said quietly. "I have seen it, long since." She inhaled deeply and slumped on the exhale. "But it's one thing to mentally see and understand it, quite another to shake off more than half a lifetime of conditioning."

"I know." Touched by her weariness and vulnerability, Derek drew her against his chest and put his arms around her. "On a lesser scale, marriage to Margo conditioned me into thinking that every beautiful, intelligent and ambitious career woman is as singularly undomesticated, unmaternal and uncooperative as she was. Knowing you taught me otherwise."

"But how?" B.J. leaned back to frown up at Derek with genuine confusion. "You've seen what I do to a kitchen. If anyone can be termed undomesticated, surely I'm it."

"Uh-uh. You're untutored, unskilled. But you're willing to try. Margo never was."

For the first time in days, B.J.'s sense of humor surfaced. "Trust me, Derek, even with tutoring I'll never become a June Cleaver."

"I'm not asking you to."

"And I'm no Mother Goose, either."

"Maybe not, but you will be. Kids adore you."

"What do kids know?"

"More than you think."

"Derek, let me say this, please." B.J. framed his face with her hands. "When I was seventeen, I was diagnosed with endometriosis. Doctors still aren't sure what causes the condition, but in my case the upshot of it is—and on this every doctor I've spoken to, agrees—I can't get pregnant."

She stroked his cheeks, putting all the love and tenderness she felt for him into this simple caress. "You are wonderful with children and you deserve to have as many as you can handle—"

"And I'll have them," Derek interrupted. He caught her hand and pressed a kiss into its palm. "With you."

"But—"

He covered her mouth, first with his hand, then with his lips. He kissed her until she stopped struggling, then raised his head. "You and I, Bertha Joanne, will adopt."

If he had said, "You and I will colonize Venus," Derek doubted B.J. could have looked more nonplussed. Delighted with her reaction, and quick to take advantage of her slack, rounded mouth, he dived into another kiss, which involved tongues and teeth as well as lips, and which soon had her full cooperation.

That's when he withdrew once again and waited until B.J. opened dazed eyes, before saying, "I'm still waiting for a answer, you know."

B.J. knew when she was licked. In truth, she had never in her life yearned to be persuaded to an opposing point of view as she had wanted to be persuaded today, by this man. By Derek. To be able to spend the rest of her life with him, to be his partner, his lover, his wife. To be a mother... the mother of *their* children. And they would be theirs, those children, even though they'd be adopted.

Happiness pervaded every nook and cranny of her being until she thought she would burst with it.

Mischief pricked her. "Umm... would you repeat the question?"

"No."

"Well, in that case—" she leaned forward, dropped a quick kiss on Derek's mouth, and smiled sunnily up at him "—my answer is, yes."

"Well, hallelujah!" Derek lifted B.J. clear up off the floor and spun her around before toppling with her onto the bed. Pinning her to the mattress with the weight of his body, he kept smoldering eyes fixed on the silvery blue love lights in hers. His hand tugged her silk shirt out of the waistband of her skirt and delved underneath.

"Now, Bertha Joanne," he growled, his fingers insinuating themselves steadily upward and leaving a trail of scorching delicious goose bumps on B.J.s quivering, sensitized skin. "Where were we, the last time we lay like this on a bed...?"

Epilogue

Two years later...

Whistling, Derek reached back into the car for his briefcase, then strode briskly toward the front door. It opened before he had even touched the handle. Experience had taught Derek to stand aside. Baby came noisily bounding out, followed at a run by Justin.

"Hi, Dad."

"'Lo, sport."

Justin, in turn, was followed at top speed by Susanna. Three years old and going on thirty, the bright-eyed and apple-cheeked Suzy no longer even vaguely resembled the pitiful bundle of humanity B.J. and Derek had rescued from an overseas orphanage the previous year. Smart, energetic, precocious, she was her older brother's biggest fan, as well as the light in B.J. and Derek's life.

"Hi, Daddy."

"'Lo, princess."

Shaking his head, chuckling, Derek watched the trio streak around the corner of the house. Contentment warmed him like a blanket—life was good.

He went inside, calling, "What does a guy have to do to get a kiss 'hello' around here, anyway?"

"Walk straight ahead, that's all."

B.J. stood with arms wide and lips puckered just inside the door. Their kiss was leisurely and thorough.

"Hmm," Derek murmured, nuzzling his wife's neck. "A man could get used to being greeted like this."

"I'll just bet he could." B.J. relaxed against him, relishing the moment of unhurried closeness. They usually had to postpone times like this until after the kids had gone to bed. "Got a letter from Starburst today."

"Oh? How's she liking Reno?"

"In a word—*her* word—it's fab."

Derek nibbled on B.J.'s ear. "Fab, huh?"

"Yup." B.J. arched her neck to better accommodate her husband's sweetly marauding lips. "Hmm," she sighed. "Don't stop."

He didn't for quite some time, and it was only because the kids might come barging in at any moment that, with their arms around each other, they reluctantly headed for the kitchen instead of the bedroom.

Working side by side preparing dinner, B.J. brought up Starburst's letter again. "She says she, uh, *ditched*—again, her word—that Lester fellow and is now living with some man named Mac. By the way, are we ready for another baby?"

"She's pregnant?"

"No, *she* isn't. Not yet, anyway."

At that evasive reply Derek stopped breading chicken breasts to watch B.J. competently shred cabbage for cole slaw. "So?" he prompted, when she neither looked up nor stopped what she was doing.

She gave him an innocent look. "So what?"

"So are we ready for another baby?"

B.J. picked up a carrot and slowly began to scrape it. "You tell me, darling, are we?"

Derek laid down the meat and rinsed his hands at the kitchen faucet. After drying them, he took the carrot and the vegetable peeler out of B.J.'s hands and laid them aside. Then he gripped her shoulders and turned her to face him.

"All right," he said, "something's up and I want to know what it is."

B.J.'s eyes, meeting his, were glowing with a secret light. But a hint of mischief lurked there, too. "What makes you think something's up, Mr. Coleman?"

"For one thing, Mrs. Coleman, I just realized you got home before I did. Didn't you have a conference with Schreiber Consulting today, and didn't you say your mother would be here baby-sitting?"

"Yup, sure did." B.J. beamed up at him. "I was done at two."

"But you didn't come back to the office."

"No, I went to see Dr. Phillips."

"Phillips?" Derek frowned. "We go to Dick Kravitz. Who's—?"

"Ob-Gyn."

"What—?"

"Babies, among other things."

"Ba—" Derek choked on the word, tamped down an irrational surge of hope and searched his wife's eyes. What he saw there instantly sent hope soaring again. He swallowed. "Bertha Joanne, are you saying—?"

Eyes brimming, her smile radiant, B.J. nodded.

"Sweetheart, are you sure?" Derek asked hoarsely. "You mean to tell me we...*you*...?"

Again B.J. could only nod. One second later, locked tight in her husband's embrace and melting from the heat of his kiss, she couldn't even do that.

* * * * *

Silhouette
ROMANCE™

NEW COVER
Coming this September

The Silhouette woman is ever changing, and now we're changing, too.

Silhouette Romance has a new look, but inside you'll find the same heartwarming, satisfying love stories that emphasize the traditional values of family, commitment... and the special kind of love that is destined to last forever.

Look for the new Silhouette Romance cover this September.

When it comes to passion, we wrote the book.

Love has a language all its own, and for centuries, flowers have symbolized love's finest expression. Discover the language of flowers—and love—in this romantic collection of 48 favorite books by bestselling author Nora Roberts.

Two titles are available each month at your favorite retail outlet.

In July, look for:

Search for Love, **Volume #11**
Playing the Odds, **Volume #12**

In August, look for:

Tempting Fate, **Volume #13**
From this Day, **Volume #14**

Collect all 48 titles and become fluent in

If you missed any of volumes 1 through 10, order now by sending your name, address, zip or postal code, along with a check or money order (please do not send cash) for $3.59 for each volume, plus 75¢ postage and handling ($1.00 in Canada), payable to Silhouette Books, to:

In the U.S.
3010 Walden Avenue
P.O. Box 1396
Buffalo, NY 14269-1396

In Canada
P.O. Box 609
Fort Erie, Ontario
L2A 5X3

Please specify book title(s) with order.
Canadian residents add applicable federal and provincial taxes.

Summer Reading At Its Best

In July, Harlequin and Silhouette bring readers the Big Summer Read Program. Heat up your summer with these four exciting new novels by top Harlequin and Silhouette authors.

SOMEWHERE IN TIME by Barbara Bretton
YESTERDAY COMES TOMORROW by Rebecca Flanders
A DAY IN APRIL by Mary Lynn Baxter
LOVE CHILD by Patricia Coughlin

From time travel to fame and fortune, this program offers something for everyone.

Available at your favorite retail outlet.

Silhouette Special Edition

You loved the older sister in
The Cowboy's Lady,
you adored the younger sister in
The Sheriff Takes a Wife.
Now get a load of the brothers in
DEBBIE MACOMBER's new trilogy.

continuing in July with a

BRIDE ON THE LOOSE!

Jason Manning was shocked: Charlotte Weston was the first woman to accept his slovenly ways, like sports... and love him! It wasn't until Mrs. Manning—eager to marry off the last of her sons—planned the wedding as a fait accompli, that this bride took off at a dead run!

You won't want to miss this last book in Debbie Macomber's trilogy. Only in Special Edition.

If you missed *Marriage of Inconvenience* (SE #732) or *Stand-in Wife* (SE #744), order your copy now by sending your name, address, zip or postal code along with a check or money order (please do not send cash) for $3.39 for each title, plus 75¢ postage and handling ($1.00 in Canada), payable to Silhouette Books, to:

In the U.S.
3010 Walden Avenue
P.O. Box 1396
Buffalo, NY 14269-1396

In Canada
P.O. Box 609
Fort Erie, Ontario
L2A 5X3

Please specify book title(s) with order.
Canadian residents add applicable federal and provincial taxes.

WRITTEN IN THE STARS

WHEN A LEO MAN MEETS A GEMINI WOMAN

Seth Danner's daughter was the single most important thing in his life—until he hired beautiful, vibrant Margo Rourke as his new housekeeper. But Seth had no way of knowing that Margo's secret might destroy his family....

Will the power of love bring these people together? Find out in Suzanne Carey's **BABY SWAP**—the **WRITTEN IN THE STARS** title for August 1992. Only from Silhouette Romance!

Available in August at your favorite retail outlet, or order now by sending your name, address, zip or postal code, along with a check or money order for $2.69 (please do not send cash), plus 75¢ postage and handling ($1.00 in Canada), payable to Silhouette Books, to:

In the U.S.
3010 Walden Avenue
P.O. Box 1396
Buffalo, NY 14269-1396

In Canada
P.O. Box 609
Fort Erie, Ontario
L2A 5X3

Please specify book title with order.
Canadian residents add applicable federal and provincial taxes.

SR892

 Silhouette Romance ®